Broken Whispers

life and times of a pavement prostitute

Bob DCosta

Ukiyoto Publishing

All global publishing rights are held by

Ukiyoto Publishing

Published in 2022

Content Copyright © Bob DCosta

ISBN 9789356455788

All rights reserved.
No part of this publication may be reproduced, transmitted, or stored in a retrieval system, in any form by any means, electronic, mechanical, photocopying, recording or otherwise, without the prior permission of the publisher.

The moral rights of the author have been asserted.

This is a work of fiction. Names, characters, businesses, places, events, locales, and incidents are either the products of the author's imagination or used in a fictitious manner. Any resemblance to actual persons, living or dead, or actual events is purely coincidental.

This book is sold subject to the condition that it shall not by way of trade or otherwise, be lent, resold, hired out or otherwise circulated, without the publisher's prior consent, in any form of binding or cover other than that in which it is published.

Dedication

Who shelter behind walls

And take refuge in backyards

Where piss and clay-cup whiffs blend with

Your sad homes across the border

And your aged parents whose body failed to trek across,

For you, this book, with love and respect…

Come you masters of war
You that build the big guns
You that build the death planes
You that build all the bombs
You that hide behind walls
You that hide behind desks
I just want you to know
I can see through your masks

Like Judas of old
You lie and deceive
A world war can be won
You want me to believe…

Masters Of War, **Bob Dylan**

Contents

I Am Ghungroo, A Refugee	1
I Name Myself Ghungroo	7
Ghungroo Meets Her Beloved	10
Sold By Her Father	18
Sold To BSF Guard	26
Run, Girl, Run	39
Escape	48
Border Country	52
A Walk	60
Nocturnal Life	64
Michelle, The Mongoloid	67
To Be Or Not To Be A Prostitute	75
Whore Street	84
The Dagger	89
Ghungroo And Michele Cafe	94
The Terrorist Customer	98
Fire And Shelter	102
The Tea-shop Poet	105
Prison Cell And Game	118
An Explosion	125
Conversation With Foetus-bro	127
Dad	132
Back Home	138

Dad at the Window	141
The Speech	144
Slogan On Walls	148
Little Happyland	152
Ill Health	158
Mother Love	162
A Marriage	164
Eastland Is Happyland	174
The Other Dimension Or Ghungroo Dies	180
Ghungroo's Spirit Lives	184
About the Author	*187*

I Am Ghungroo, A Refugee

Prologue one

Everywhere there's autumn smelling in the air, and all over in the streets of Calcutta. The memories of the evening draped by the golden colours of a sunrise have tired me, and these are the memories I have in my mind as I declare my love for this confused city – the queen of the country if you are a lesbian, and if you are gay then the city is a male, and if you are none of the above – that is, you love the city because it's a city where you were nurtured, then you love Calcutta because it's nothing but Calcutta, the city whose contrasts vary from the few skylines determining to rip the skies to the pavement dwellings flattening the metropolis, because you know, loving your city is synonymous to art restoration. The city where even the mad man of the street quotes from Tagore's Gitanjali to Shakespeare's King Lear, the city whose colossal, old and ruined mansions boast of art in their flowing rhetoric.

A soul full of boiling ramshackle words snuggle inside, and a sorrowful gust of fatigued summer breeze tell my thoughts, and there's the aimless 21-jewels water-resistant blue Citizen watch ready to tell my future, and the old blind woman of the pavement of Lower Circular Road. She treats me like her son whom she had lost in the Naxalite reign of terror in the early roaring seventies. This stone-faced cop, he questions an unlicensed whore outside The Lighthouse cinema hall and as I sit on the roadside boulder next to the narrow winding lane where a play of faint light from the mouth of the lane and some glow from the last hut inside cohabit, these faint unconscious patches of glow mixed with the darkness squatting forever within churns my thoughts. And as the dull brilliance lures me over the uneven squelching pathway, the sudden scream of a woman reaches my ears, and I aimlessly walk and peep through the small niche of a window of the shack strewn with wretchedness, only to find a woman throwing her legs up and kicking in mid-air, she is in constant fight against the male power dominating over her. When I resume my seat on the boulder, a boy of around eighteen has cupped his hand to the tap and he cools his throat with its sweet water. As he stands up, satisfaction spreads its soft comfort on his face, and soon after he turns towards the rickshaw, and stepping inside the wooden handle of a frame, lifts his vehicle and resumes pulling it, the small bell tied around his finger striking the wooden handle with a mechanical *ting-tung-tak, ting-tung-tak*.

Blood runs down the streets, *ting-tung-tak, ting-tung-tak*, down the gutter, *ting-tung-tak, ting-tung-tak*, even bathing a ten-rupee note that slipped out from the hand of the lady of the street as she was throating out the final stanza of her baul song, *ting-tung-tak, ting-tung-tak,* her song of torn souls beyond the border. E=MC (power of 2), where E is the emotion, M is your Motherland and C is the Constant love for your country. This lady taught me this, the power of love over all kinds of power in this universe.

Ting-tung-tak, ting-tung-tak.

Somehow the picture of a grandmother-old lady appears from the bag of memories, her head covered with white hair, a few streaks of blackness peeping from the straight receding white. She has lain her head on a footstool, it is a one-inch high footstool, and she folds a piece of cloth and places it on the footstool. And this acts as a cushion. She lowers herself on the mat spread on the floor of the open verandah and gently rests her head on the improvised pillow. This open verandah of her one-room hovel becomes her open *bedroom,* and it is vulnerable to rodents that scurry up and down the drain below her *bedroom.* She had spent many an evening rocking a little child in her lap, and at the child's insistence repeated the song over and over again, but she always wore her smile, never did she show irritation, and the song *Ten Children* took the little child to the forest of the song and the river bank where each of the children played about, and at the end of every stanza, one child would either die or get eaten up by a beast or fish till finally the last child was left lonely, the half-a-song child, and he began to shed copious tears till his intense loneliness and immeasurable sorrow took him deep into the woods – from where he never returned for r*eturn* was unwritten in his blood. *Why did he go away, why did everyone leave him, why was he alone.* These thoughts, all along, plagued this person as a child, and it still does.

Strange, that in summer, autumn lays hold in the city; and strange too that memories come of the evening but tinged with it, it's the golden colours of a sunrise that has tired the city.

Ting-tung-tak, ting-tung-tak.

(from the diary **I am Ghungroo, a Refugee of the Bangladesh War of Independence)**

Such was the condition when Ghungroo arrived in Calcutta and this condition continued even after she became a prostitute of the pavement but she didn't know that I was somewhere around her for I sometimes rested in her mind and sometimes went away on my usual strolls.

Prologue Two

This is not a prologue, but
a pact between you and me

Before I begin to collect my notes, before I arrange the pages, number them page one, two, three, let me tell you, my friend, he is coming to take me away. He stays close to my residence, and has never broken his promise.

So that you trust me, so that I will go without any regret, I have taken this task of arranging these sheets. And as I do, I will read out to you, to ensure that if you have some doubts, some questions playing hide and seek in your mind, you may feel free and ask me, I will clarify them. Thus, after having heard the journey of my life, you may give me a clean chit, clear me of blame and erase any doubt from tugging at your conscience. Because this happens to be the first time, I have ever hidden anything from you.

There, on the little cane table, your favourite pizza, Neapolitan Pizza, ordered online from Dominos counter, New Empire. They have topped it with tomato, garlic, oregano and extra-virgin olive oil. I insisted them to add two slices of bacon, your treasured salt-cured meat over it. So that as you listen, you will take bites in between and sip orange juice prepared in the fruit-juice mixer by me.

I Name Myself Ghungroo

Ghungroo's POV

I renamed myself Ghungroo:
One small anklet bell rolled down the table,
a sweet sound.
And within my tiny heart the gentle far-away peal
stirred a feeling strange
a feeling defined, undefined,
a *no* and a *yes*
and the anklet-bell music played in my ears
captured the heart.

I still remember the bountiful man gifting it:
fishing it out from his pocket,
unwrapping the pealing toy
holding it close to the closeness of my ears.
Once snuggled there, he shook it.
PEAL-PEAL
PEAL-Peal

peal-peal
peal-eal
eal-eal...
like a temple bell
floating in the mist
the gentle far-away sound, a balm
soothing the mind.

And with the sound of *ghun-bell* chime in my ears,
I moved about
in my little room
that day
on the pavement, dancing a jig
muttering the name in my mind
to my brother
foetus-brother, residing in my head.
Click-clacked my tongue, I,
every now and then
and a mixed feeling of pleasure
and no-pleasure
coursed in my veins
on my soft cheeks danced

with the name I had rechristened.

And thus was born
Ghungroo.

*

This part of the pavement unlike the rest
muttered I
the best
and my muttering approved it
the sleepy sparkle in my eyes adored it.
And when loneliness closes in
the smell of music tingles at my nose-tip
lingers over my dusky skin
the peace attached to the sound
a reminder of childhood days back home.

Ghungroo Meets Her Beloved

Ghungroo's POV

In the air hung always the smell of the pavement
and through the folds of the bamboo-strip walls
it wafted
and into the pavement dwellings at times
and on the floor of one such shack, I flopped,
eyes to the world outside
through the many little openings on the walls.

The picture of the guitar lady, at the window
strumming into the stained-glass-window soul
into the flight of broken-winged birds
returned through the flimsy cracks of my mind
and also of the tune soft, the rhythm of a river lazing between two shores
a reminder of my mother dead, killed by my father, alcoholic

but my mother's song

Two birds on two shores/ In the middle quietly a river flows

alive and kicking always in my mind

and now the strumming lady alive in my mind.

And when I was moving about, bundle in my arms in this strange city

 a soothing sound reached my ears

and I looked up, and there,

at her window of alone-ness, sat the Mongoloid-featured lady

and something whispered then, out of my heart

and touched the lady's.

And now inside the shack, in two large steps I could easily pace up and down

but I sat where I was sitting

on the debris of depression

and I waited, but my waiting bore golden apples

for unknown to me

the Mongoloid lady,

the guitar lady

had followed me.

12   Broken Whispers

The simple intricacy of horizontal and vertical bamboo strips

helped me pick someone walking

down the pavement edge

and I waited, waited for that *someone* to tap

and when Michelle the Mongoloid tapped, not exactly a *tap* it was,

but as if a cat-scratch at the door

scrape of its claws on the bamboo skin, scratch-scratch stop.

Scratch-scratch-scratch stop. And scratch again.

"Cat-scratch," I later recalled, a smile-jig at the corner of my mouth

and my eyes.

And when Michelle pushed the door, hid I myself behind it.

My lips pressed, my emotion suppressed, my hand stretched

and out flowed my feelings

when holding my beloved's wrist

and I pulled her inside with an all-gentle feel.

Pull-Gentle

Gentle-Pull

Gentle-Gentle-Pull-Pull.

And as a flower rests its head on the leaf

allowed Michelle herself to fall into her beloved's waiting arms

and Michelle's apple-size breasts *hindranced*, and when this comment

reached my ears, smiled I again, and sat in a restless calm

the smell of hibiscus oil in my hair

and a swoon swaying with an occasional swoon

unbalanced somewhat Michelle's mind

and didn't she know that?

Soon were we on the cane mat

and drawing out a transparent plastic packet from within my blouse,

I lit the *beedi*.

Love at first sight it was, for Michelle and me

Michelle, my ideal companion, with mute sparkles in her eyes

and the sleeping sunlight in her hair.

We sat

we spoke

we didn't speak.

And we smiled at times.

And when all inhibitions fled from our souls, we looked:

she within me and found a strange orange glow

and I within her for Michelle in Michelle.

And the more I looked

the more Michelle's island captivated me

and the palm trees hushed me to silence

educating me to an overwhelmed dream of a thousand rivers

and in me rode the silence of autumn with her

and I knew if I hadn't strummed the strings of love residing in Michelle's heart,

I hadn't done anything

If I, Ghungroo, haven't brought

the sorrow of the morning dewdrops in my palms

I have done nothing

And if I haven't felt the syllables of the songs

of the broken-winged lark

nothing have I done
and if I haven't felt the night-queen fragrance of anyone's solitude
and I haven't pained anyone to bring out her song
I have done nothing.

On the mat of cane we lay down, friend with friend
lover with beloved.
Michelle with me; I with Michelle.
And the stars smiled
our palm-lines joined
Michelle's life-line with my fate-line
and my life-line with Michelle's fate-line.
And two love lines pressed
softly
with early love
and first joint-moistness.

We were strangely true,
we were not truly strange.
And we spoke a strange language.
Languagely strange.

16   Broken Whispers

In the land of solitude sometimes we met
the hole large enough
for love's breath to enter
and at times the two of us met clothed in our dreams
and in mine we flew over forests of love
a forest ground with trees and glens
and above, forest sky with dots moving and circling
planets on irregular orbits.

And in Michelle's dreams
the pair bathed in the golden waters of a sunset
with tiny sparkling ripples
the glee of the lovers' hearts showing
and the setting sun warming us
and in turn warming the water.

And a strange language was born
out of purity and love
our love, in whose beautiful pit at first sight
we had fallen in
and needed water and sunshine.

No other time spelt appropriate
than then, sculptured together.
Silently.

Sold By Her Father

Ghungroo's POV

The disquiet moans of the nightjars came through the closed window of my room,

the day I was sold, and in the wakeful trance of a quiet baby kicking the air,

I sat up on my bed counting backwards – *364 days, 363 days, 362...*

and the nightjars sang in a moaning rhythm.

And over the freshly wilted flowers my eyes moved

as whispered I, "I am seventeen years

and three hundred sixty four days old today."

The teak-wood smell of the bed

and the burnt-wood smell of the hookah fallen on its side

and the red terracotta smell of the dancing figurine

all blended in the midst of an intellectual orgy

when my words punctured their poses.

"And tomorrow is my birthday, and today
at three in the afternoon
the day will wane
the wind whisper in my hair
at dusk."

And when my breath completed the sentence
and it softened the glint in my large kohl-black eyes
and the smell of dying embers rested on my semi-full lips
I shook my head and murmured
Did I ever come across this mixed feeling before?

I click-clacked my tongue
ran my fingers over the hair-line cracks of hills and valleys
on the faded white walls.

I was the pianist gliding my fingers over the black and white reeds
with drunken artistry
over the piano of pain
pain I could see hovering

black and white

pain I could smell

black and white

and pain I smiled back to

and click-clacked my tongue.

Father on the stringed cot in the front yard

father who lifted his head

from his favourite chipped-at-the-rim china tea cup and father who said,

"You need to work for the family."

Father whose eyes held unfeeling words

an untouched bowl of thick bland soup, the surface hardened and crusted

into a frosty field.

And hobbled out from the kitchen, mother

thin in frame, her left hand holding

her large pregnant stomach, her right hand the metal ladle.

And the fumes from her eyes stood between her and father

readying for an everyday war.
"No. She won't."
And paused she and breathed deeply.
"She'll study
yes. An air pilot she wants to be."

But this time the noise of her gritting teeth
gnawed inside father's brain
the fangs of the wolf's decision penetrated deep
and clamped at his hopes
and into the hare's throat sunk deep.

Father sipped once more and threw mother a cool level stare
over the rim of his cup
over the rim of his wrath
and in slow measures he stood up.

"So the head of the family here are you, eh?
Except in stories I didn't know any other boss really existed."

He put down his cup on the cot's brown frame

and he rested his hands on his hips

and all the while his eyes locked into hers.

And before the black rolling clouds in the sky

burped out angry growls continuous, he took three steps forward

and he touched her hair.

"Who's the boss?"

And uttering that, a mighty push father gave her.

Watched I mother falling

watched I mother's reflexes

thrusting her hands out to her bloated belly

her pregnant stomach

with a sharp dull thud hitting the floor right where the abstract art

of the copulating monkeys lay unfinished.

Watched I all this.

And the nightjars crooned their moans from the neem tree.

And the light outside was a washed-out grey and it stuck

to my throat with the unspeaking cold stare of a sadist

as my eyes widened and I cried out *Ma*.

But the *Ma* squeezed itself

into a pepper ball

and in my Adam's apple lay wedged.

Mother on the floor

mother unmoving

mother spread-eagled

mother more than a wasted human.

To the left her head tilted, offering her right cheek to her husband

for the deed he had done

and I saw her jawbones, smooth

standing out tight and hard

and her lower lip, pale

now *A darker shade of pale.*

And guttural sound seeped out of her throat

– she, Beethoven's ghost playing *Guttural Sonata*

on a sea-sodden piano.

On mother's stomach rested my eyes
and blood was a quiet flow
of death oozing out from between her legs.

On mother's chest my ear, my mind scrounging to define
the indefinable silence
at the door of her little unreliable red machine you call heart.
But my ears captured my seventh-month old
little unborn brother's squeals fading,
fading inside mother's little-big dark universe called womb.

Not dead am I said the squeal
said the foetus, *Shaken and only stirred,*
and jarred am I, from life
not broken away.

A sound of whisper my ears picked up
a soft rat-a-tat through the headphones
of a moving train heard for deep sleep

now reverberated inside my head
this slow metallic vacuum-hollow music.

And something stirred within.

The slight-warm nerves in my brain
turned a little warmer,
my seventh-month foetus-brother, my foetus-bro,
with the slim pinkish-white frail thread of his hands and legs
pushed his sibling's hair
and then inside my head snuggled he
slow and sure, before a comfortable position took he
mewing to himself
tears misting his closed eyes.

Cradling a pint of rum
and dragging me over the rough country road
father threw me at the terrorist agent's feet
collected the money
and left over the swaying path.

Sold To BSF Guard

Ghungroo's POV

"You little *randi*, you whore," barked the agent under his breath,

and in his hut he clawed at my dress till the only piece

was the strand of tired thread over my belly button now pressed

by the abdominal sweat of his desire.

He slapped and watched my copper complexion

turn a darker shade

and he laughed a coarse laugh

and rejoiced at his growing passion.

My eyes closed

I continued humming the moaning tune

and when my voice began to fade into the growing night,

from the neem tree the nightjars took over

and they blended my humming with a tone of moan

the mourning of my country under brother-enemy's hands

holding bayonets of wrath.

And exhaustion took over.

The bitch moans and sings I overheard him say

I use force and she sings the song of widows' reunion under street lights of sadism.

I place her hand over the candle flame's heat and she holds it there

moaning and singing baul songs

of broken sunsets.

My body a little fortress, and on the battered fortress

grew the brownness of pain

morning, soft brown

afternoon, softer brown

at dusk more-brownness brown.

And with the guise of a jungle-dog black-brown mind

when darkness crept in

on the little domes of the fortress

scars of abstract art appeared

its slim pillars of thighs un-spared

and on the mound of the waist appeared they
and to the slight right of the belly button
in browns and dark greens.
When the sickness of molestation sickened the agent
after days, the politicians joined the cue
the vultures in them dipping and raising their ugly heads.

In my head my foetus-bro whispered
Bend but don't give up, sis.

And *Bend don't give up* became my mantra for the night
and food for the day
and the silent beads of revenge, the caress soft and soothing
of my brother's cloud-soft breath
worked the formulae.

And the nightjars sang it, and they carried it along.

Ninety-nine nights later, over pathways broken and forested

and brambles and snapping-under-my feet branches,
he dragged me.

My steps faltered and when I stumbled, a swarm of bees hit my brain

and their melancholic buzzing shattered my cells.

Money passed hands

and I, bread from starving men's hands

from one to the other.

Dragged me they to the border post

and over a bottle three-fourths empty

two military-fatigued men sat

on their lips a military-march tune.

The first one swayed, and the first one left,

the other removed his drunken rifle, unbuttoned his shirt,

and when he loosened his camouflage trouser with the dagger-holding belt

and unzipped his mind

he aimed a smirk at me, his scar running faster down his chin

and at his master's commands the scar smiled a wicked smile.

Quiet down I told the dragons of worry and fear appearing in my mind

and when I whispered to my foetus-brother

his lump-sized head appeared, eyes closed.

While the man was doing what he was doing,

and the sweat of his chest wetting mine,

my hands caressed at his neck,

the shoulder blades, then down.

My hand crawled to his waist; my magical fingers curled

around the handle of the dagger by his side.

And I waited for his mind

to blow out the silky-slipperiness

of his bodily desire.

And when that happened too soon, my orgasmic hatred

a slow and steady cheetah

gripped and plunged the knife into his neck.

Faster than the speed of lightening it found the artery at his throat,

Gash!

Gash!

Then the semi-circle slash.

And when half-hearted drunken-growls filled the room,

and his stretched hands clutched at the air, and his hand fell down limp

the silent and huge world under the marble sky spun on a sudden

and it went on its heels.

And it was then the art of dying birthed into a dance

in eighty-five degree angle

and my mind crackled crumpling paper balls.

My mouth formed into *Blowin' in the wind* in C Major.

And while the man fell in the slowest of slow degrees,

I belted out:

> *How many roads must a man walk down*
> *Before you call him a man?*

And when I came to,

> *Yes, and how many times must the cannon balls fly*
> *Before they're forever banned?*

his eyes from horror turned into a more resigned horror

and when on his last few seconds on earth, the portal of fire opened

felt he the charring heat on his skin

and the song turned his mouth into an artistic twist

of eternal cruel rest to his soul.

Soldier of the jungle, you, said I,
the song has soothed you.
Never again will you perform this act.
Eternal death you have attained.

Life is a dagger,
death is a song.
A piece of truth
and the chilly wind
rewinds itself to the moon
at four minutes past seven.

And before the day wanes,
return me the time and rewind it
so my window can spy the moonbeam

you robbed last night.

From the corridor of my song, I stirred awake,
and my eyes in a vague focus set on the blood-dripping blade
opened their petals in slow degrees
from a nine hundred ninety-ninth dream
of doves and mutilated passion.

I nodded at the obedient weapon:
"Dagger," my breath swore
"you my friend from now on
my poetry come true."

And I touched the blade to my lips.

Proud of you, dagger, and on his camouflaged shirt,
I wiped the blood

The slowness of the approaching dawn
pushed me to peep, and there, down at the corner
under the mahua tree, in a mahua-induced sleep
lay his colleague.

But the world closes around me, and a black hole I'm falling into.

I slip

I slide

I go hurtling down the slippery slope.

Where am I?

Am I being punished? By whom?

Please help.

I only defended myself, Lord.

If you want stifle my heart.

Tie my hands.

But please let me go.

Let me run away

from these murderers.

Are they dead?

I don't know…

Another BSF lay on the ground, swayed his head, snake-like

from side to side.

Drunkenly asleep, he jabbered in endless fashion

to his drunk mind

while I crept forward, the hilt of the dagger gripped in my hand

the dog murmuring, his eyes closed.

I stretched my hand above his head, in slowness raised it

lowered it down

but stopped midway.

Foetus-bro: Stab him.

Ghungroo: But he's sleeping, see.

Foetus-bro: Harmless are sleeping men

drunkenly-asleep men more harmless.

Just three stabs. Yes.

One.

Two.

And three.

At the throat.

Ghungroo: Forget it.

I turned away.

But a few steps when I took

paused I, and turning around, came back

and while I peered down his thick-set jaws and tiny closed eyes

and the burnt-brown tanned face, I worked on a blob of saliva

spat it out on his face, next.

I chopped my hair into a boy's size and shape
and when I threw the last bits into the air
a voice touched my ears; soft; a whisper.
I turned here, there.

"You look smart..."
My heart leapt out of my mouth.
"...sis, whatever,"

I smiled a faint smile.
My brother.
My bro.
My foetus-bro.

"Mother is no more," he whispered, his suppressed tone

caressing my ear drum

soothing me

calming me.

"But see, you and me. Always together. Since then."

I smiled; I nodded, I tapped my head, his residence.

I looked around. *Is the left the right direction? Or the right?*

On a sudden a vice-like grip my hand felt.

"You can't escape me, lady." The BSF drunken guard smiled,

his mouth exuded the smell of illicit liquor.

I jolted out of my brain.

"Please. I'm not a prostitute. Please leave me.

I have been kidnapped here. Help me. Please."

My words did something to his brain:

the neurons began to stir and whisper something

and he cleared his throat, wiped his mouth with the back of his hand

and swayed his mind in rhythm.

The five-second silence dragged to a thousand and one minutes.

"Ahead are huts on the left, the cremation ground the landmark

to your right. I'll be in the last hut."

"Thank you." My voice was a whisper of gratitude.

"Come around seven in the evening.
Now go back to the hut you came from.
Through the wall surrounding this walled city of ours
is the only way to escape."

Run, Girl, Run

Ghungroo's POV

I peeped from behind the door, my hand gripping the dagger hilt.
Past six and darkness descends from the sky,
and sprawls over the trees, first in grey
and soon the leaves will take a darker grey.
The moon peeps from behind the clouds.
Night, throttle the moonlight. Hide me in your dark cloak.
My heart goes thump. And thump.
My little bag is ready under the bed.

A salwar and kameez and a thin sheet like a shawl
some biscuits in a poly bag
and a bottle of cold water
and the eight-inch long dagger.

Will Kishor be true to his word?
A cloudy sky is eternally unpredictable.

*

Stay calm, stay calm.

I picked up my packet, took the few steps to the sitting room.

The main door on my left

the door to freedom.

No, escape.

First *escape,*

followed by *freedom*, if at all you are successful.

A sensation. An intuition. The door is ajar.

Someone standing.

A shadow falls on the wall.

Foetus-bro: Why are you saying all this?

Ghungroo: What can I do? At times you are a stranger lurking in my brain.

I placed my feet softly on the floor

lest the soft pats stirred awake

the ears of the house.

I pulled the latch and its rusty voice squeaked

in irritation for waking him from his siesta.

Outside it was dark.

I peeped to my left and right.

Dark were the patches where the plants and trees stood,

And no one around.

In a flash and as noiselessly as a cat, I closed the door,

laid the weight of my body on my toes, clutched my bag,

I hurried down the left flank.

The path was dark.

Thank you Darkness.

And I bent and ran.

A light run, more of a jog, but a quick one.

A jog-run.

On my right, lights from the windows of the home for the aged appeared,

and from my left the smell of the night queen flowers floated.

We had one in our yard next to the tulsi plant.

Mother and I would run a needled thread through them

and make garlands.

That is the strength I will carry with me.

The field appeared vast and stretched,

the moon had pushed the clouds away and she was up in the sky,

and I exposed.

And if found out, perhaps the only virgin orifice

I'll have left

will be my left nostril.

I smiled a grim smile at my own joke,

it twisted the corner of my mouth.

But Kishor would lead the way to my freedom

the employee will go against the employer to extend help to the captive.

I dug my hand into the bag and out came the watch.

Mayaji's wrist watch, a spare one

I had pinched from the room I was given to sleep in

and where all the caresses and molestation (they call it *anointing*) had begun.

The time two minutes to seven.

There, ahead, stood the girls' huts

Mayaji used them as products.

Faint lights from their windows followed by darkness

of the cremation ground helped me pick the last hut.

Yes, that last hut was my destination.

That was what was told.

I stopped outside the door, my breath coming out in gasps,

I straightened up and taking a deep breath, tapped.

A face and curly head poked out. The door opened further,

and Kishor's eyes fell on me. I peered above his shoulders, stepped inside,

removed my footwear and allowed my naked feet

to fall on naked bricks.

Smell of incense crawled into my nostrils

And a bed covered with a blue and white checked sheet.

Two pillows side by side.

A clay goblet stood on some bricks

to the left corner of the door like a pot-bellied child Buddha

sunk in deep meditation,

making a massive effort to attain nirvana.

I looked at Kishor, and he at me. The corner of his mouth sparked a smile.

"You might be wondering why I'm doing this

why letting you go."

I only looked at his face not allowing any passion to rule on it.

"I've done some wrong in life. No more."

"Thank you," I said, my voice breaking into choking gratitude.

"Well, ready?" and his gaze fell through beady eyes.

My eyes shifted from him to the door, an indication from me.

"Let's get on with it," he said, his voice steady.

I turned, taking two paces towards the door,

stopped and looked over my shoulder.

He stood standing where he was

his arms by his side, his thumbs dug into his trouser pockets

a look of a man on holiday dancing in his eyes.

His face turned to the bed, then at me.

A gleam in his eyes.

I was supposed to read his mind. *That is not in the agenda.*

He took two steps towards me, then tapped his left foot.

His breath fell on my face, the smell of bootleg drink,

exuding through his tobacco stained teeth.

"First," and he pointed at the bed.

An insulting smile lighted up and he covered his mouth.

That's some decency after all.

The roof of my mouth dried up, the saliva on my tongue suddenly evaporated.

The mouse has easily fallen into the trap.

Holding my hand, he pushed me,

and my shoulder blades and buttocks

touched the mud wall

and its coolness crawl-slithered up my spine.

His face came closer and his mouth rested

on the softest part of my neck, the artery.

He bit into its softness

like a modern day vampire

ran the tip of his tongue

over the green nerves.

For a few seconds my breath stopped

then released

stopped

released.

My mind spun, comprehending his riddle.

The meaning appeared in a flash:

Nothing comes free.

You fulfill my desire and I fulfill yours in return.

To cite a cliché: You scratch my back, and I scratch yours.

He turned me and, with his hand on my shoulder,

pushed me towards the bed,

as if I was with sight leading the blind

from door to door. For alms.

No, door to door for sex.

As if a door will open,

and I will be taken in while he will wait outside

tambourine-ing with the aluminium begging bowl.

I told myself: Ghungroo, your head is now on the chopping block,

why worry about the axe.

Time was chained to a sack of loaded bricks

and stones.

"Here it is," Kishor said, pointing at a particular part of the wall.

He parted some branches "Straight down and across the fields

and then two ponds away, the path you have to take." He paused.

"Beware of terrorists in the village-town.

And some virus in the air."

Escape

Ghungroo's POV

Eyes darting here and there, I picked my feet,
first through shoulder high grass
then lower
till a glade appeared in view.
The road ahead rejoiced at my sight
for trudging down the roadway, far ahead
a crowd
of men and women
and women and children
walking.

Melted I into the crowd, into the soft clanging of their pots and pans.
"Leaving our country," said one. "Our land taken away
by West Land across India. They want us East Landers
to take up their mother tongue as our national language.

And kill us and kill our mother tongue.
But how can we stab our patriotic song.
Not dirt it is you wash away from your clothes.
Our language, it beats in our veins
even when we cry, laugh
cry-laugh
laugh-cry.

Daggers use the terrorists as pens.
Guns as toys
on all on us.
The West Land government sends soldiers
to shoot and kill, to rape our women
to play hide and seek." She paused.
"So let us cross the border, you and I
and step on the border neighbour soil."

An the old lady offered puffed rice.
Thanks, murmured I, teary-eyed.

Soon a station, the platform empty and dark
and some slashes of light from the moon overhead
through the leafy firmament.

We boarded the train. Destination *Safe Land*, my ears picked.

Dim light from the ceiling,

refugees crowding the floor

between the seats

and stuffed smell of people's perspiration

and a quietness of death in the air

and these the ingredients of fear trapped in your heart.

The train shuddered like the man bound to the pole

in our town

the angry flames from the torch

licking at his body.

My head swooned

my shoulders loosened

my breath came out slow

and a sudden whisper, "You've done well..."

and my heart leapt into my mouth.

I turned. But, "...kudos, sis,"

said in my head my brother,

my foetus-brother,

my foetus-bro.
"But see, now you and me
mother no more
but you and me
together always
since then."

I smiled, I nodded and tapped my head
where he resided
and swooned again.

Border Country

Ghungroo's POV

My mind heard colours and my third eye saw sounds
when out from the embraced arms
of the train's rhythmic lullaby I came out
and the chaos of displaced people were eleven panting horses
bearing the weight of the universe on their shoulders.

I dragged myself out of the station building
and the humid air caught my throat by surprise;
and the carcass of a cow in the middle of the road
its stomach burst open where maggots wiggled about
in complete freedom over the putrid flesh.

My brother nudged me then, *listen.*
Listen to the sounds of yelling and screaming
rending the air around you. More refugees
– like you – arriving.

When passengers spilled out and an organized chaos followed
and some cursed four-letter words
in their queer language twang
and they ran helter-skelter and out of the station
it happened
yes, it happened.

Into a vomit of anger enlarged a policeman's eyes,
his mouth opened
and closed in fits and starts.

Yes, that's what you'll now say, you son of a pig!
What could the government do, eh?
He spat on the floor.
You people begged.
Don't you know
your country is
the Begging Bowl of Asia?
And on an army of flies on the pavement
he spat out a large blob of saliva.

And now your country will become
the Begging Bowl of the World.

And when the policeman said this, it happened.
My mind whirled and colours zoomed in and out:
And Tagore, with a bamboo cup in his Parkinson's diseased hand
leant against the unwashed wall
next to the fruit seller.

And in the midst of herbal wine sips
the poet looked around and whispered
"Lose yourself" in his washed-out voice
of the Padma River
and with the turbulence of pride flowing from her cherubic hair
and standing nearby
appeared The Rani of Jhansi
puffing at a stale cigar and tapping her feet to the song.

Judge Joshi joined
and joined Einstein soon

scratching his beard.

And from his *khadi* silk kurta breast pocket
the former pulled out the Chinese fountain pen
and he reached towards Einstein
and signed the verdict –
to this city's short and long term portentous future –
on Einstein's pink guitar.

And when the poet came to:
He's nervous, but on the surface he looks calm and ready
To drop bombs, but he keeps on forgettin'
What he wrote down...
each of them walked up, and took the pen from the Judge
and put their signature, a surety
to the few days left of this dying state
and its city.

Sound of metallic crick-crick of feet
and there the nightjars perched on the tram car wires
adding music to Eminem's lyrics
 with their husky flute-like moans.

And hand in hand Chanakya
and the dysfunctional Bhagwan Rajneesh appeared
and they crossed the road and joined the motley crew
of human moderates,
pinching Aryabhatta's cheeks
and offering their signature.

Then on a sudden, it happened.
Einstein, he turned his head
and his eyes glued themselves to mine,
and our mental vibes reached a common level.

I asked, *Is this surely to happen?*
What all is being sung, is it really true
or are you guys taking us for an eccentric spin
down the rabbit hole?

My head swooned as Einstein gave his assertive nod,
and the song faded and Tagore and his band
reached a smoky and distorted position.

Out of the confusion and crowd a loud sound shook the air.

The explosion flung refugees all over. An old lady's body
hit the far end
of the station wall
and her head blew off.

A boy's body struck against a tram car
and his father's body
pounded against a school wall.

By now my head began its spin again
and darkness descended
in slow degrees.
Knew I not where I was
only that the terrorists' reign of terror
was inscribing a different history
with the refugees.
My murmurs turned to silence
and I began sinking once again.

I stirred; I opened my eyes
and my brain in chaos, I looked around.
The pavement began to crack into potato wafer bits

and from the ground they floated
and half way,
nausea churned in my diaphragm,
and hollow emotion filled the lungs,
my ears felt the surrounding indistinct noise
and clamour
of hurrying people
hurrying faces.

The humid-sticky breeze struck my face.
A tube well at the pavement edge quenched my thirsty hunger
And scattered rubble from demolished buildings defined the street
sneering at me.

The immune system of the city's rules
was hanging
on the tram car wires of slap-happiness.

Among the thronged refugees everywhere my eyes fell
among the crowd one face I wanted to avoid,

or meet face to face. Would I be in bliss if I could remove him from this world?

Not a total bliss, but bliss of a kind it would be.

Heaven would be mine, if I could remove my father.

Father.

Loathe I that word. Detest it I, precious to daughters.

And then, like a pressure soda-bottle style

releasing from the tiniest-of-the-tiny opening,

like smoke from weed escaping with a gentle stubborn attitude of sorts,

my reality-marked swoon-of-a-dream

seeped out of the brain, pushing it out in all its slowness.

A Walk

Foetus-bro's P.O.V.

I lay huddled in quietude in one corner of the throne
– Ghungroo's mind.
Splashes of vague marks on her face,
some kind of wearisome-ness stamped below the eyes
squatting in a stubborn stain.
And her mouth open, also bare proof
of the condition pacing in her mind.

Go for a walk, I nudged
else the claustrophobia
closes in around you.

Once in the open, the sticky-with-humidity breeze
slapped her face
and the silent street
punctured with stench
attacked her nostrils.

On a wall ahead a board with the words Mid Street
and she stopped below it,
and her eyes at the board,
she murmured,
"This blind alley is a lie."

She looked at far-away distances, beyond the houses across,
beyond the horizon and as far as her mind could take her.
Her eyes were somewhere, yet, nowhere.
Then, like a sudden zephyr, they spied at the window.

A lady.
Straight-haired.
Mongoloid featured.
Slimness slithering on her skin.
She held the guitar stalk,
rested the plectrum
and gently swept it
over the six long slender wires.
And when she touched them,
and tiny ripples of water quivered.

A beautiful sound birthed out, reached into Ghungroo's ears,

a piece of music.

The words married the music, the lady whispered out the song

and it went on and on

the words

till the end came, fading the words and music.

The lady tilted her head backwards

rested it on the wall next to the window,

and all the while murmuring something.

Her whispers,

silent prayers,

secreted a juice of ease

and in the unhurried manner of a fakir's walk

down the corridors of his thoughts,

her murmurs put her mind at rest.

Her eyes closed,

opened the wings of a soothing rainbow.

The voice and her strumming,

woke something up in Ghungroo,
something indefinable,
and something flooded her mind.
And in the cocoon of these thoughts she lay
stood up
and with the world of her bundle of a bag,
began trudging again.

Nocturnal Life

Ghungroo's P.O.V.

I moved on
into long sewage pipes of concrete,
into long sewage pipes huge
had they stuffed their bodies
and crammed their minds,
the refugees,
unfortunate.

I walked ahead, and when night appeared
and swallowed the splash of dusk
I dragged myself into a blasted building,
and fell on soft damp leaves.

At night, nocturnal life woke up into existence:
The scuttle of a bandicoot
across a bed of dry leaves
and that scurry-scurry-pause, scurry-scurry-pause

of a lizard darting out its tongue at insects
and that unbroken slithering-hiss
of a snake.
 I was the weakest here, in this forest.

And with their tiny of the tiniest pincers
on my legs ants bit
and for endless days
cockroaches found my cheeks
to feed upon.
Rats and other rodents
they nibbled my hands and legs.

I was Gulliver; chained by *weakness;*
food for a starving nation
the Aryan race, the animal kingdom
and before sitting down to feed on my entrails
the Nazi salute,
Sieg Heil,
they gave.

In delirium was I
but aware of two responsibilities.

One: Sleep. Sleep. Sleep.
Two: Eat the wind.
Divided by four twenty-four hours equal six.
So, sleep for eighteen,
eat for six,
the six not at a stretch
but whenever invaded the pangs of hunger.

And now you know all, Michelle,
my Michey,
at the window you were strumming,
singing,
and your Moonlight Sonata
invading my veins.

Michelle, The Mongoloid

Foetus-bro POV

The guitar lady's eyes fell on the hordes on the pavement
across her house.
And she stopped short in her tracks.

How is it possible that so many are out on the road?
I was at a dead end, you know.
The words of a song made quick entry and exits
and once they came, they were all bundled up
like *silence trapped inside the mind like a caged animal.*
And I needed to pour some water and sunlight
into my creative flower pot.
But the scene outside tripped me, threw me headlong…

Yes, people seated on the pavements,
and their belongings kept next to them
– cloth bags and utensils and pots and pans.

And some of the children, their heads on the bundles,
fast asleep.
She had never seen a refugee multitude of this kind
and so decided to sit down on the cobbler's wooden box.
Some washed their faces from the tap
at the corner of the pavement.

A few men returned, their hands gripping bricks
and when they placed these next to each other
two ovens sprung up,
and very soon a sparkling fire was born
in the womb of the oven.

Her eyes travelled from one scene to another
And it fell on a young lady sitting on the edge of the pavement,
hugging a small bundle
her white shirt streaked with dust and dirt
her black skirt turned dusty.

She sat in the island of her own loneliness,
her face hugging a far-away look.

Something stirred within the guitar lady
and it was an indefinable feeling.
Her mind was an emptiness,
and it churned a slow whirlpool dance.
Have I been able to locate what I had lost?

The feeling that she was again drugged
into song-like dreams was like a passion
she had experienced once
and with this,
her thought became her companion
for the rest of that day.

In the evening
she went out and her eyes once again fell
on the pavement people,
the pavement taking in squalor –
 a contagious disease spreading its arms
to welcome
the refugees.

More improvised ovens sprung up

and more bundles
covered the pavements.

And more children were born as refugee children
instead of growing
from babyhood to childhood.

The kids ran around
and so did the filth and dirt
they seemed to have been birthed with.

And she plodded on.

Retracing her footsteps, the guitar lady found,
a little ahead of the market, piles of bamboo strips
lying on the ground
and someone's head down
busy.
And nearer went the guitar lady,
this someone fitting horizontal
and vertical strips onto each other.
The same white shirt and black skirt.

Footsteps on the pavement,
the young lady turned her face
the other smiled
and she bent down,
stretched her hand.

Quite soon two lattice walls –
a smaller wall, a door,
and one more, bigger than the wall –
stood ready.

Ghungroo and the guitar girl
put up the walls,
the ceiling and the door
and a plastic sheet attached to the two top ends of the door,
became the curtain-door.

The two of them stepped into the now-created hut.
"I am Michelle," a soft voice said,
and a light smile lit up the lady's lips.

"And I am Ghungroo."

Seven that evening. Michelle stood outside the curtain-door
and scratch-knocked.
But once was adequately sufficient
for the door was ajar
(she realized this only after knocking).
and the street light fell on the floor
in all its yellowness
of an egg yolk,
and this faint light picked up someone on the floor,
her left arm resting on her side,
the right
jutting out from the elbow in a horizontal position,
the fingers lightly curled into her fists.
Michelle coughed a light cough.
No response.
A louder cough,
(loud enough to sound only inside the room)
but it brought no stir.

The straight-haired lady's heart skipped a beat
and she stretched her hand,
she touched Ghungroo's shoulder

and she shook it with all gentleness.

A few seconds floated here and there,
and when the gentle shake was applied again,
the arm stirred a bit,
the hand picked up the movement,
the fingers twitched an extent.
Stirred! She has stirred!

Ghungroo opened her eyes,
and they peered into the darkness
(unable to fathom the unknown land
of the living),
she turned her head around,
and her silence asked,
Why, and how come this faint honey-glow.
Michelle smiled, sat up,
extended her hand.
Ghungroo held her palm, the first stirrings of smile
woke up on her lips.

She stood up, a picture of frailty painted on her state,
eyes still droopy,

back hunched to an extent from the shoulders,
and hair awry.
Scars of hunger stuck on her cheeks,
and every faltering step screamed
with ravenous pain.

To Be Or Not To Be A Prostitute

Ghungroo's P.O.V.

On the floor we lay, eyes at the convulsive ceiling, the delicate wind

up to mischief, and it picked up speed with a huff and a puff,

and it lifted the ceiling's soul and within seconds brought it down.

When this dance continued for a while,

my fingers tap-tapped to the ceiling sound rhythm.

The Sound on the Ceiling,

doesn't it ring nice?" said I in broken English.

What, and Michelle looked up at me.

On her forehead came up a crease

and she nodded and I wondered,

and she gauged my life's journey here

in this unknown border country.

Would it be like the flimsy ceiling?
And soon we laughed
when she placed her hand over mine.
and I turned my hand.
And now our palms joined, I offered it a soft squeeze.

One night here was eternity, a cast-away land,
a stow-away land, a one-week hours' land.
Michelle with mute sparkles in her eyes fell into quietude,
and she sat by my side, silently understanding my silence.
When I murmured to no one but myself,
she smiled a casual smile, a part-of-life smile.
And in this world of the pavement hut, next to me someone sat.
When singing a *baul* song to myself, she sat,
when conversing with my bro, she sat.

And as days passed into nights, and nights into days,
I slept and hollow-coughed
I hollow-coughed and sat up
I sat up and paced about the room.

And when I walked about, I hollow-whispered,
and hollow-murmuring, and murmuring and whispering
I sang a *baul*-song.
And Michelle's presence entered my system
and she became a part of me.

A few days soon, I turned my head and rested it
on the nineteen year old girl next to me.
On my knee I tapped my fingers,
a song in my lips:

> Lalon fakir every moment says
> One who loves knows
> My soulmate's words he listens to

Michelle repeated the words, and she murmured them after me
and from a reclining position our voices stood up soon
and she matched her voice pitch to mine
and the song reached a slow swim in a lagoon,
and curved our mouth into a happy tilt.
In this one-room house I became a presence,
as she became one too

till we were a presence to one another.
Our palace this pavement hut, this hovel
and our days and nights chalked in one-ness.
 A Saturday it was and something was arriving,
with its hands something brushing away
the little obstructions; the little-heavy things
that something
elbowing away,
kicking away with its legs, the obstacles.
The bombs and guns, and the daggers
of the impending war
our eyes over the bigger obstructions.

That morning, I read the text message
the pale sun's smile brought:
CHANGE your LIFE.
CHANGE the way you THINK.
A slow waltz the message did in my mind
and on my face it glowed.

No money, no food
and for two days

we drank water as food

and when we starved, we put our mouth to the tube well

and drank

and drank

and quenched our hunger.

And when the day was waning

And the refugees were half dreaming

And the eastern sky was darker than our motherland

on a sudden said Michelle,

Money the petrol of life.

And in the room the humidity weighed her words.

Work.

Yes.

That's important.

"A maid I shall be," said I. "Don't you worry. Or at *The Pice Hotel* work."

My words a peeping-in and peeping-out of my head did.

And on Michelle's forehead the creases appeared three.

"Your dusky skin. Your fine hands," and paused she.

"They are meant not for you to be. I can do that, not you."

Her tone was a lazy river.

To hers I took my face close.

"What why, why not

you think so?" and a whisper-word it was.

"No one knows you here," whispered back she.

A whisper-word contest.

And she yawned at the floor and the floor gazed back at her.

"To build trust it takes time

and it needs to be cultivated.

I'll work instead."

I put my hand on Michelle's arm.

"No. Don't. As it is, you are spending money on food."

"No darling," paused she. "No money now. People know me.

Work comes easier

to the known."
And her fingers over my hair did a stroll.

"Ok," and I paused. "How about…"
My mind paused
a longer pause.
My mind's door was ajar.

"How about what?" enquired Michelle's eyes.
Her voice stood up faster from the lazing tone,
an edge of anxiety and excitement, the whisper-word contest
down the drain by now.

"How about customers? You get for me?"
my voice a soft mist.
"We both work. Together."
And I squeezed her arm.

She fixed her eyes at the ceiling
and merrily swung the silvery cobweb string
when and Michelle nodded.
And Michelle paused

and nodded again.
She waited for the traffic signal of her mind
to change from red to green.

"Rich customers are rarer
than a chance summer rain," said she.
"We have to be lucky in roping them."

My eyes still on Michelle's face, I nodded a strange nod,
the nod possessed not only a *yes* but also a *no* in it.

Michelle's eyes fixed on the floor
when my idea churned slow in her brain.
Her face changed colour around the cheeks.
She nodded
she got up.

"Yes," said she and her eyes sparkled like the first tiny flame
on a sparkler, the *phool-jhari*,
when lighted.
"There's this place, The Mahal."

And she gently squeezed my dusky arm.

Our enthusiastic voices floated about in the room,
sometimes my soft husky voice
followed by Michelle's soothing whisper,
each overtaking the other.
At times hers and mine slipped and blended into a symphony
of lesbian-lovers' refrain,
the same-sex love refrain,
the mermaid-lovers' serenade.
Our planning, a marathon race
faster than Pheidippides.

Whore Street

Ghungroo's P.O.V.

And beside me stood Michelle at the crossing.

Stand and rove your eyes to your left.
Stand and rove your eyes to your right.
Front.
Left again.
Then to your right once more.
Then stand and stand.

But not for long.

My eyes picked a man sauntering down,
looking here, looking there.
We stood
at the end of a by-road,
a concrete path towards a clump of trees
and the dead end of a moss-smeared wall,

and damp and slime.

Ahead lay sprawled, like a wounded man dead,
the main road
but activities, busy doctors, in full throttle.

At the nerve centre of activity, Michelle loathed standing.
Crowds of people moved about,
in and out of tea shops,
in and out of a provision store.

Not a manufactured product
was I,
Michelle said
and in the market advertised for sale.
"Not you.
Not a slave chained
and displayed with a price tag
are you.
A dignified business, this.
You trade your flesh for money.
As respectable a job as any other, it was."

This man approached,
Michelle took a few steps forward.
"She's good, *saab*," and she looked at her beloved,
her voice a professional tone,
but with an air of
accept-if-you-want-it-doesn't-bother-me tone,
pointing her forefinger, all the while, at her beloved.

The customer eyed me up and down,
and even his trouser didn't fail to eye-watch me,
nor his hands for they began to twitch,
nor did his extra limb for it began to stir,
but his *paan*-filled mouth gaped
and the *paan* juice
yearned to tongue all over me.
His eyes rested on my twin orbs,
his mind trapped into the apples,
his mind,
now taking over,
lapping the juice.

When my eyes met Michelle's.
she nodded,
nodded a smile, *Go, baby, go.*
And Michelle's eyes watched as the customer and I
walked towards the brothel
some fifty yards away.

When close to the dingy two-storied building,
the black-trouser-clad man almost savoured me
with his eyes,
but when we vanished up the wooden stairs,
his greed for me opened,
opened further all its pores

I removed my kameez,
and rested it on the cracked back rest
of the old teak chair.
It moved, rocked on one of its legs short by some centimetres.
Out came the *salwar* next and rested on the crude seat,
and when my bra followed,
it nearly popping the customer's eyes out of their sockets

and barely had he rested his mouth on my neck
when my eyes fell on his clothes on the chair.
From his black trouser pocket peeped out
a black and white photograph
and a familiar face looked right into my eyes.
The gloss in the photograph hit my eyes.
The smooth forehead, slight curly hair
loose over the head, moderate rounded lips,
eyes like a doe's, a sharp semi-long nose.
The picture churned in my mind; tightened my body.

The Dagger

Ghungroo's POV
No, Ghungroo. Relax.

Down my belly the customer's hand travelled
and my nerves I loosened and relaxed.
My hands stretched towards the chair,
inside the room the hovering musty-ness
now loosened
trapped my nostrils.

My hand, inside my bag,
the fingers curled around the dagger hilt,
and as the customer's maddened brain
poured out his silky and slippery vision,
the metallic blade of my dagger
found its destination:
His throat.

Jab and pull.

Jab and pull.
Jab, jab. And jab.

The warm feel of blood on the blade
and the nerve
throbbed on my little finger
a slow dying fire, the blood.

The penetrated knife,
his thin helpless hands clutching at the air
stood a clear vision in my mind,
and in no time his reflexes slowed,
his life breath ebbed away.

I jumped up,
took the picture from his trouser pocket
and down the stairs rushed
two steps at a time.

The deserted street was still lazing.
My body rushed on hurried feet.
My mind flew.

Michelle, there, at the tea stall

and on the table my voice tapped with the finger nails.

"Let's go," whispered my voice, and my hands motioned her.

Michelle stopped sipping, l

ifted her head from the clay cup, mumbling,

What the fish?

"Where?" enquired she. "You look tensed."

"Somewhere." I took my mouth close to her ears.

"That man. The customer. My father sent him."

My puzzled face slapped her.

"You sure?" her mind in the maze still.

"He... he had my photograph."

Michelle stopped short, eyes fixed into mine

and she swallowed

and my words

swallowed her voice.
Whole.
My hand inside my bag, she looked at the bag,
at the hand-lump inside.
And the image
of the curved blade and its dead-metal gleam
and the wood-brown hilt in her eye balls reflected.

And I looked at my beloved.
I read her thoughts.
I dug my hand inside the kameez
and out came some currency notes
trapped between my breast and bra
and placed the five of the ten notes
into her palm.

She eyed the money,
and a faint smile appeared.
From the customer? she meant to ask.
Her mouth curved into a smile, and she hummed:

> *Suzanne takes you down to her place near the river*
> *You can hear the boats go by*
> *You can spend the night beside her*

*And you know that she's half crazy
But that's why you want to be there…*

Ghungroo And Michele Cafe

Ghungroo's POV

Legs pulled together, her chin on her knees,
from the corner Michelle watched me,
her fingers tapping to the rhythm of another song
as she continued preparing the weed,
caressing the little leaves in all artistry.

The prepared stick lit, the sweet burnt smell coiled
and it spread all over in the room.
And into a smile my face lit up.
My hands waved
at the dispersing smoke, flapped them towards myself.
In thick coils wherever the smoke hung,
my face went closer,
and I inhaled, my eyes closed.

I displayed innocence, and Michelle smiled.

The glow on her face, a child's when he is given
a balloon.
She is getting normal.
Michelle pulled at the stick and she blew out a lung-full of smoke,
and when she passed it to me.
I placed my mouth on hers instead,
sucking at the smell lingering in the cave
and the floating coils my tongue touched
and it licked the smell
and I desired a part of the smell to linger in my tongue,
the capturing smell of faintness
with saliva mingled in equal measure.

I pulled deep at the weed-stick,
took the smoke for a long tour down my throat
and into my lungs,
and on Michelle's lap my head rested.

"Say something," Michelle whispered
and I turned my head, looked at her
in a vague sort of way,

defined my own ambition, the abstract but sure ambition.

"For some reason, I can't fathom my own father
wants to sell me…" I whispered, releasing a coil of smoke.

"…and send hired men to kill you," Michelle added.

But let us forget it, said I
and she said then "say something, something different…"

And I cleared my throat:
There's a house called Doors, but in reality it's a mere house with no doors.
It is your open mind unlocked from within.
And when hours of work frustrate your brain,
it's then at late evening your home welcomes you again.
But today you open the drawer,
you feel the chill of steel in the grip of your soft hand,
the forefinger on the curved comma of a trigger.

And when the nozzle caresses your temple just where the pulse throbs

yes, throbs like the breath of a baby,

and your finger squeezes the comma

and the soundless plop of the rushing bullet meets you inside your brain,

enveloping you with its sweet soul

and as you slump to the ground the ghost in your brain gives a suppressed laugh,

"Welcome to Ghungroo & Michelle Café,

for work is for the lesser mortals,

and here you can relax."

I stopped. "This," I said,

"is the definition of the Jupiter trip

with Kerala Grass."

And Michelle could only stare at this lady, mouth open,

her words injecting a trance of hypnosis.

The Terrorist Customer

Foetus-bro's POV

I lay in my sister's head, and something tingled in my brain,

the smoke uncoiling in a drunk-monk fashion.

Ghungroo smiled, and to the smoke she spoke in a whisper-smoke voice,

"This, the definition of a Jupiter trip with Kerala Grass."

Michelle stopped in her tracks, staring at me,

mouth open, her words injecting a soporific trance,

her soul in mystic dance.

"Yes," said Michelle and nodded a slow nod. "You don't need blood there,

and no weapon you need.

All in peace. Nothing in pieces."

And nodded they as Ghungroo edged closer to Michelle, the lady, clasped her throat she gently

And she pulled her in lovingness

and Ghungroo's mouth on hers rested in religiosity,

and her tongue searched for the Jupiter Peaceful.

From the brick shelf Michelle took the small plastic container

and on Ghungroo's eyelashes applied *kajal*.

And in the midst of the makeup, a scratch-knock at the door

a noise from the curtain-door,

and when soon a hand pushed the curtain,

a man's hand followed by his face framed the opening.

His face, fair, big

and somewhat flat with curly hair adorning the head.

Slim and tall was he,

and a picture of boredom marked his eyes.

From one lady to the other his eyes moved,

and it stopped on the spot

of kajal on Michelle's little finger tip,

for she was moving it

with the stroke of an artist on her beloved's lower eyelashes.

And like an autumn wind,

she swept a thin stretch of black cloud

over the horizon.

And my sister's cheeks glowed with a touch-up of pink,

and her lips coated with a faint red lipstick

Michelle had bought

for her inamorato.

My light brown complexion stoked something in the man.

He took two steps forward,

allowed his pocketed hands to fidget about.

My eyes fixed at him,

the pacific shade spelling my calm thoughts.

"Today no sleeping," in an audible tone whispered sister

"But other things."

The man smiled, nodded and two ten-rupee notes

dropped he in Michelle hand.

"*Sir*, it's fifty for sleeping," and Michelle looked at his face.

"And forty, for other needs."

His left sleeveless forearm the man rolled up,

and my eyes fell on the letters CM tattooed on it

And now they tattooed themselves into my mind.

"Be happy, you should," said he. "Offering something, at least."

And his voice slowed and gruffed all over in the pavement hut.

CM. Chinu Mannu. He belongs to Chinu's insurgent gang.

I unbuttoned the man and a film of satisfaction
spread over his face.

Fire And Shelter

Ghungroo's P.O.V.

We locked our hands loosely and we walked, we looked into each other's eyes

and at the kites sailing in the air

and when Silence interrupted our little silent conversation,

"Look. Fire," someone yelled

and we dashed.

Our pavement hut on fire.

Flames of red,

orange

and yellow

leapt here

leapt there,

on the bamboo walls.

And the plastic roof no more a roof,

only a hollow hell.

The fire a Hide-and-Seek player on the lattice,
and it ran in from one diamond-shaped space
and rushed out from another
chasing imaginary gnomes and fairies.
Our work of love transformed to a hot-ash bed,
a smouldering smoke house.
All the fires of hell compacted
and let loose here.

Past eleven at night
and the market ahead.
Hard drops of rain threw themselves in slants
and it brought the neighbouring pavement people
into the market shelter
and crates and boxes lay covered with plastic sheets
and in the midst of running cats and dogs
stale smell of rice sacks and lentils,
the pavement children moved about,
some leant their weary bodies against rice-filled sacks,
babies with their breast-sucking mouths half open
lay in their mothers' laps, drenched in sleep.

And empty fruit crates filled with stained clothes
lay in whatever corners they could find,
and a smell of dampness prevailed around them.
On puddles of stagnant drain water and potholes
mosquitoes sat,
and some flew around and landed on people's skins.
A bandicoot paused for a split second midway
on its path, looked right and left in nervousness
and scurried away.
A few cockroaches crawled out from behind sacks of rice,
their antennae studied the vibrations produced
from people taking shelter.

And under such a sky, we were beggars and not choosers
we were the stars
shining in that firmament.

The Tea-shop Poet

Ghungroo's POV

"Hello Biplab," and sighingly-sighed Michelle
and she looked up at the figure,
gaunt and tall.
Chiselled jaw, and cheek bones,
the six-foot of a man who threw
a silent gaze
and his head gave a wise nod.

"You are a poet I told her," Michelle said,
and he laughed a conscious laugh,
and sideways turned his head,
and met my gaze.
Something in his eyes,
it could calm even a raging tempest.

And with the poet's medicinal gaze the pain on my shoulder

became a receding sea.

"No. No. Only a poet of sorts,"
and he *ha-ha*-ed back at her
and then looked at me again.
"A tea-shop poet."

"Well," said I. "Come to tea. Make our hut a Poetry Hut."

I offered him the small cane seat, the guest's throne
and while we sipped,
he had composed a fiery poem, said he, on the problem
the refugees were facing.
And all throughout, goggled Michelle's eyes
at the transformed atmosphere
from a hut to *The Poetry Hut*.

And when he had gone
I felt a tinge of pain rising within.
I looked at Michelle
and she was still in a daze.

Jealousy spread its tentacles
and coiled around my heart.
"You like him," said I
in an affirmative tone, "it seems."

Michelle rested her eyes on me,
but her mind was not in the room.

"Everyone likes him. Don't you?" she said and smiled.

"No. Yes. Yes and no," I said, my hand over my shoulder.

Foetus: She likes him.
Ghungroo: No. You can't say that.
Foetus: Why? Her cheeks blushed.
Didn't you see, and her eyes widened?

Michelle smiled, she went to the brick-book shelf
and pulled out a book.
"See, Biplab gave me this. On my last birthday."

The first page said:

Twenty Love Songs and a Poem of Despair
Pablo Neruda.
(In Biplab's handwriting)
Michelle, on your 20th, this book.
A humble poet, Biplab,
21st July, 1970.

*

In Biplab's house gathered the intellectuals,
and we sat on the cane stools.
Most on the bed, the ladies' sarees
spread around their feet,
round colourful carpets of soft orange, green.
And three chairs, rickety and dark brown,
near a book-table pushed against the wall.
The comfort of the floor mat welcomed everyone
and others occupied the few cane chairs.

And floated his discourse between war and dream
and some nodded and others threw him a gaze,

his husky voice reverberated

in the tininess of the room.

And Shiva listened from the calendar on the wall –

Shiva, in blue, in his *tandav nritya* pose, his left leg lifted towards the right,

the *damru* in his right hand, the live snake more alive than him.

The abstract painting of a rickshaw rested in mid-air.

And the spider from the cobweb listened

from the corner of two walls

dangling in a long trickle.

And Biplab's husky voice reverberated in the tiny room:

When a war takes place, you are in a dream,

a practical dream.

You don't want the war, but the war wants you.

It wants you because without you,

the war is no war.

Without spilling blood,

without breaking into your dream

Mr War is outside the circle of his attitude.

And in his temperament when he is not,

he is not a man

only a non-existent, not even in an abstract form
but a force of sorts,
yes, a force of sorts
begins to churn in his mind.
Thus the abstract image is born,
of ruling over someone.
And without consciousness, the feeling of war is born.
And war is committed
and blood is shed.
And this blood is *she*
And this blood is *he*.
And now man can form the image
the image of devastation
and of its horror.

Even if solipsism says everything exists
because I am existing,
War has been existing
even before man had begun to think of ruining man.
The dark force has infused from nature.

The oppressor and the oppressed

lived in harmonious disharmony.

And the ruining of man had begun.

Biplab rambled on about saints fighting wars,

but the philosophy of the fight has been the same throughout history:

"I want my power to be exercised on the working class,

because I want them to follow my ideology

but they protest as they don't want to be commanded

and a clash of ego follows."

I nodded, my arm around Michelle's:

"This entire universe was born out of silence," I said.

"Silence in the void.

When we are quiet this silence appears as if in a dream

and we can only rest in the silence of silences.

By this I mean silence in the midst of sound,

because all of us were born in sound-silence.

The way this world came into being,

evolving in slow measures into what it is

and what it will be.

And look at ourselves...," and I looked at nowhere

and was speaking more to myself than the gathering,
"…when life forms in a womb, a movement begins.
This is the movement
we create in our mother's womb,
and this movement creates some sound
because any movement is accompanied with sound,
be it the slightest one.
And like a star orbiting in space which creates sound,
we too create our first and most meaningful music
in our mother's womb.

"So, friends, do not undermine yourself,
for you are no less a Beethoven than he himself.
The organized movement of your mother
– her heartbeat, her blood circulation, her footfalls,
her gaze, her thoughts –
is an orchestra to help you create your best soulful music.

And when your mother holds her new-born baby in her arms,
her smile is the best award you can get,
more than a tired sunbeam

leaning on the lost shoulder of your dream."

I paused, I coughed a slight cough
it was more of clearing one's throat.
I closed my eyes and while humming all the time,
put my hand to my waist and from the folds of the salwar kameez
pulled out gently two small thin slabs of stone
and I placed them between two fingers,
and with eyes still closed,
began striking the two slabs against each other
with my right hand.

The *tuck-tuck* sound created came soft and gentle,
and very soon when the music reverberated
in the valley of the room,
my voice sang out.

The group made no movement
and even the walls,
the chair,
the table and the bed
and other things around

stopped in their movements,
their ears clinging on to the lady's voice
and the words of the song.

> *I know not who I am.*
> *Thought I was the water*
> *till it dissolved somewhere*
> *when I said, "I am you."*
>
> *Thought I was the air*
> *but it passed by without a caress*
> *to my thirsting soul.*
>
> *Thought I was the sunrise with its shafts of fire*
> *but they soon melted into a morning of miseries.*
>
> *Thought I was the bleeding sunset*
> *but soon it turned into a dungeon of sinfulness.*
>
> *I know not who I am.*
>
> *I know not who I am.*
> *Thought I was the earth*

till it loosened itself with my touch
and scattered into the desert of my desire.

Thought I was a Hindu
but remembered words form the Quoran.
Thought I was a Muslim
but words from the Geeta touched my soul.
Thought I was a Christian
but words from the Granth
caressed my heart.

Thought I was from Sri Lanka,
from Afghanistan, Bhutan,
from Bangladesh, Maldives
from Pakistan, from India, Nepal
but every song perished half way on its journey
every step faltered
every lake dried up
when my eyes rested on them.

The mosque closed its door
the church its gate
the temple its portal

the gurudwara its entrance.

I moved over unknown paths,
and rubble and stones.
Debris gave solace to my soul.
My feet bled,
my throat parched,
and my blood coursed slow in my veins.

A light appeared in the distance
when my fatigue closed the lids of my eyes.

At last I found the answer in my begging bowl
the bowl of the fakir,
The Seeker…

I stopped and looked at nowhere
but the entire room resounded with my words.
Some members nodded in approval, some smiled.
A slow clap sounded from somewhere.
There was no one whose palms were not striking against together.

Some sort of connection held the words of Biplab
and mine.

Cobweb strings were they

dangling from the corner of the two walls.

And when tea arrived in clay cups,

and everyone sipped and chatted in soft tones,

but Biplab held his cup, and I held my cup,

my hand rested on my thigh, my mind travelling.

Was this a new path of love?

Prison Cell And Game

Ghungroo's POV

From my hand the paper fell and the pages flew in all directions.

My curses louder and they rippled over the river Hoogly

flowing merrily under the Howrah Bridge.

The urchins giggled to their heart's content and the monkey leapt there and here.

One sole page flew towards me and finally stopped at the feet.

Read I in broken English:

    DISEASE, HUNGER AND DEATH STALK

    REFUGEES ALONG INDIA'S BORDER

    Sickness, hunger and death

    are common scenes now along the border –

    unofficial figures put the number over five million – have

    fled the country to escape the torture of the fascist government...

Then after a few lines

> *...The fleeing people have brought cholera with them. Official figures put the death toll here in the state at 3,600 but reports indicate that it is much higher, probably well over 5,000...*

> *Here in this Indian town near the border, a mother had died of cholera an hour before, but the infant, less than a year old, continued to nurse until a doctor came upon the scene and pulled him gently away...*

Of death and destruction
of hunger, disease and death
I come across the news every day
of my country across the border.

The weather touched with cool fingers
my skin
and sitting outside my shack,

I closed my eyes.

On opening them,
a grey pall hung in the air,
penetrating into the red earth-coloured Tagore statue.
The day my father had sold me,
a similar weather reigned,
like the announcement over the radio
of a possible air raid
from the terrorist-government
of the border country.

Sound of purring
and a police jeep turned the corner,
stopped outside our hovel,
and three white-uniformed men and a woman got down.

My throat parched,
I breathed deep in and out.
Steady Ghungroo. Steady.

They looked at us,

came forward:
Who is Ghungroo?

I pointed to myself.
The sturdy female police stood by me,
a quiet steady glare in her eyes.
The remaining three stepped in,
one upturned empty buckets,
the second rummaged through the pile on the table,
the third through the contents inside.
Out came hair clips; hair band; tiny bottles
of red lipstick; bangles; cigarettes; a packet of weed
and condom packets.

The three's head turned and they gave a professional gaze around.
And when dissatisfaction stamped their faces,
they demanded if there were any weapons
I was hiding,
and it would be better if it was handed over.

They threw another suspicious glare,
-- not finding the dagger –

they handcuffed me,
jeep-ed me in and sped away.

At the far end, in the police station
a muscled man of law sat.
The lady poked and prodded me
into a washroom
and "Strip," she commanded, pushing me.

I hesitated, closed my legs, adjusted the *churni*.
"Remove your kameez, you bitch," snapped her voice,
and a resounding slap flew and struck
my cheek.
My head swirled,
black and blue blazes of light danced,
and the force behind her hand shook my name out.

"You whore, we have enough evidence
you have blood
on your hands."

Two well-built women suddenly entered,

and aimed the fat bulbous hose on me.
And the sudden rush of icy water hit me
and its force threw me down.
My persecutors' giggles and laughter was a strange evil song,
mixed with the rough music
of the rushing water.

The room dark, and a faint light flooded
a dirty yellow glow on the wall.
My abdomen throbbed with convulsive pain
as one by one several of the men
entered the cell
emptied packets of rubber
threw them on the floor
and threw themselves over me
on the bed.

My mind, uprooted from the jungle of inhumanity,
a piece of driftwood, flung into the sea
by a cyclone
of physical and mental torture.

I prayed for my beloved but no one arrived.

And when the faint light of the morning appeared on the East
the door clanged open
and I dragged myself towards the exit
Biplab and Meghna Roy, the NGO lady
who looks after two old age homes
and three institutions for the welfare
of street children
stood in the police station.
And Michelle's eyes fell on me,
she raised her hand to her face, her eyes enlarged,
and tears welled up.
And she rushed forward, her sobs blending into my ears.

An Explosion

Ghungroo's POV

I smiled to myself.
The refugee children nutritioned
with my and Michelle's efforts
and Michelle's shower of love too
during my absence.

At the crossing,
I turned left and into an open grassy patch.
A few people sipped tea
from the tea stall at the entrance.
Some refugees under the pale sun
and others came forward.

We gathered around under a sprawling banyan tree
and I spoke of employment a must for refugees
when the government has decided to look after them
with food

clothing a
and shelter.

And when the gathered people nodded, and their minds
accepted the words
on a sudden the sun thundered,
the oak trees snapped out of their life
and the tiled house of a grocer
blew up
into smithereens.

Another boom in the centre of the second park
and in that instant chunks of the park
flew out in all directions and children
flung all about.
And blood-streaked bodies of the aged
lay strewed all over.
Everyone and all
streaked with blood.
And yells and screams filled the air thick.
Not a single soul stirred.

Conversation With Foetus-bro

Ghungroo's POV

While Michelle stayed back in the hut that evening
and she lifted her head from the guitar
but continued strumming Cotton Fields
I dusted the room
and placed Michelle's books at the corner,
leaned them against each other,
the last one on the left against the wall.

A particular spot on the wall stood out in prominence
with marks small,
and dark flecks on two sides on some of them.
My unfinished work.

I stepped out
looked around on the pavement
selected some scattered pieces
of little red bricks and charcoal

and mug in hand, dropped some water on the floor,
dipped the pieces of bricks into the container
and stirred them,
made a long sweep on the wall.
One followed after another
undulations.
I blackened them here,
I blackened them there
and ranges appeared out of nowhere
and the dotted birds
now flew further away from the mountains.

Below, at the foot, bushes grew
a shape formed
a woman's shape
her bloated stomach visible
and within, a foetus.

A bayonet appeared, half its blade
penetrated deep into the belly's belly
its sharp point piercing the little mass
of foetus-baby.

Blood dripped from her belly
where on the extreme right
a man stood.

And my foetus-bro looked at me, smiled.

Foetus: That's her husband. The child, me.
Ghungroo: Yes, it's you, of course, my child.
Foetus: All this running away of yours,
the refugees taking shelter at the border country.
Will it do any good?
I wonder.

Ghungroo: This escape only a temporary one.
We'll go back
(and I began on a helmet, filling it with leaves).

Foetus: How do you define *going back?*

Ghungroo: Back to your country. My country. Our country.

Foetus: And the cost in this state for that?

Do you think they will let you go,
I mean the people?
Because the people are the government
and the government
will keep you because the next assembly election
is round the corner
and they will want your favour
so they will issue you
identity cards.
Ration cards.

And the sense of security will settle in your soul
and it is then the government will tell you
cast your vote for the ruling government.
And you will blindly stamp
on its symbol
of a book
and the country's flag.
Besides, the other cost you all are paying
is atrocities.
Molestation on the refugees
by others.

And do you know
there's a spy
moving about freely here?

Ghungroo: Spy?
Here?

Foetus: Yes.

Ghungroo: I know him?

Foetus: You will find out sooner or later.

Dad

Ghungroo's POV

Michelle's dad
from the border country
and didn't that satisfy my soul?
Felt I he was my dad too
and at last after so many months my soul will call someone,
Dad.

Elation filled my soul so down the street
I went
and turned left and into the green gate
I walked in.

Up a wooden flight of stairs
and knocked at the door.

A pit-pat of feet from inside

then the noise of latch being turned

and wide open, at the door stood a white-haired man in early seventies.

So fresh

his face

so calm

his eyes.

I knew it would be you, he said,
His voice soft as falling rain.

I smiled.

I stood hesitant.

He looked up at me, his mouth open,

the skin beneath his eyes faintly dark

against his fair complexion.

His forehead broad, the three horizontal lines

three eastern horizons

of memories he holds

creased deep into his mind,

penetrated deeper into my thoughts.

He spied his border town there

with the pair of binoculars placed within.

"I was..." Michelle's father's voice was slow,

"I was at the border the other day.

It was... It was teeming with people.

Old men and women holding children's hands..."

He paused, took deep breaths.

"...As they walked, they looked tired.

A countless crowd.

Young men.

Volunteers.

Bringing order, removing chaos."

Pause.

"The sun beat down on women and children with bundles of clothes.

And packets of puffed rice many carried on their heads."

And father paused, the blank look hovering in his mind.

"I had sent my uncle a letter. That was a month ago.

But no reply."

He raised the tea cup, his hand shook.

He lifted his left hand and lightly gripped

the right at the wrist.

The shaking lessened,

he took the cup towards his mouth.

"I described my uncle to some of the volunteers.

But one of them remarked, *'There are hordes, here. How to distinguish?'*

Another one said, *'Others have asked the same question about relatives.*

But you know, it's difficult.'

And another one, *'Like a shirt button in the barn.'*"

Father's eyes were here in the room, yet transfixed

at the border

darting from here and there

searching among the millions of faces

bearded faces.

Faces without beard.

And searching right and left for that familiar face.

"I mingled with the crowd," father's voice a whisper.

And his voice travelled all the way

to the border and reached us here.

"I asked them about Faridpur."

And with the softest whisper he continued,

"I asked them about Dilauz. But no,

no one could indicate about my uncle.

He is the only one from my maternal and paternal side."

"Francis would take me for long rides on his cycle.

He taught me how to use a catapult.

I cuddled up to him when lightning and thunder ripped the sky."

And Father's voice quivered. "He was my favourite uncle,"

he whispered to the wind far away.

*

As I lay in our make-shift hut that night

the darkness took the better part of me

and I placed my palm on my abdomen.

All the past years my feeling for my own father

was different, but this is the first time

I have seen someone so lost.

This person, Michelle's father,

softens my heart for my own father.

And the feeling of forgiveness slowly coursed through
my blood.

My forgiveness came from a different realization,
I did not know his present condition –
though his agents are moving about here.
But I forgive my father on seeing this respectful old man.
He is constantly searching for a toy
but can't find it. His key to the lost item hides
somewhere in one of his brain cells,
and he probes and prods, but fails to find the key.
And seeking for the key,
this new father of mine
has become a seven-year-old.

There is no turning back. Ghungroo
You have found a dad.

Back Home

Ghungroo's POV

That night, razors swayed in slow motion
in front of my eyes.
Hundreds of them, their blades opened
and closed.
The sheen over them blinded my eyes,
an invisible master controlled them.
The city has turned into an unsafe zone.
Even the refugees are not spared.

And I drifted in and out of my thoughts.

That afternoon, after lunch
We found some shops with their shutters down
And pockets of people hanging at corners
and when I looked up
I clutched Michelle's arm:
Biplab, the Neruda of Bengal on the pavement across.

Two men stood beside him.

And they gripped his hands behind him.

And they shoved him ahead.

And while Biplab struggled, they kicked and punched him.

I lurched forward,

but Michelle held me in a tighter grip,

unlocked and unwired our door

and closed it in a flash

behind us.

And through the holey wall,

we watched with bated breath.

The thugs took out pieces of rope,

and one of them tied Biplab's waist around the lamppost,

the other one roped it around his chest.

The first thug whipped out a pistol

aimed it on Neruda's chest,

pulled the trigger at point blank range.

The face of the shooter calm,

he had done service to his society.

Bang. The second one for Biplab going against their principles.

Bang again, this one on his forehead,

out of anger and hatred against such human beings

who helped the opposition.

Biplab's white kurta splashed into red at the heart,

and trickled down.

His face painfully distorted,

his head slumped down to his chest.

Dad at the Window

Ghungroo's POV

Dad was at the window, hand under his chin, legs crossed, in contemplation

focusing on that chimney about fifty metres away.

Smoke curled out.

City mists.

Dad's mouth open

and only when I craned my neck towards his face did he see me.

And a smile spread over, in an instant.

"No temperature," he said feeling my forehead and studying my eyes.

"But continue with the medicines."

"What were you thinking of, dad?" I said and pulled the wicker footstool.

And as I said this, I spied a layer of happiness in dad's eyes and cheeks and his fingers continuously fidgeting.

"Letter from my uncle," he smiled.

He unfolded the sheet of paper, and began reading it in an audible tone.

"…Demonstrations against the government show indifferent attitude

on our safety. Insurgents breathe more freely while the common people,

people with no interest in politics are infected with danger.

The intellectuals and educationists are out on the streets.

And they are holding gatherings all over…"

Stated the letter on the grim fate of the common people

and their peaceful boat had already begun to feel the first sway

of a brewing storm

of war against terror.

"And before any peace can prevail, I am concerned of my uncle's safety." He paused,

his eyes on the paper. "And though happy, yet pensive."

Dad sunk into deep thought.

My mind buzzed.

"Is there any way you can meet him?

"How about meeting your uncle?" I was excited and nothing came out

but this wild suggestion.

He looked up, trapped into my words for a moment.

Next his face

lighted up into a broad smile.

"Yes," he said and immediately stood up

and rubbed his hands. "Why not?"

The Speech

Ghungroo's POV

At the cremation ground, after Biplab's funeral rites
some of the active members gathered.
And they selected me.

Placards said:
Support Us.
We Are Human Beings.
Help Us Not Die.

I cleared my throat, took a sip of water from the bottle. Then began:

We all know the sudden death of Biplab, the Neruda of Bengal.

Not death I should say, but murdered.

His mission was to give this speech here today

and as a mark of honour, I stand at this dais, not on my own accord,

but chosen by Biplab's loving and faithful followers.

We have to take his mission in removing the tag of *refugee*

and we have to include other objectives for the good of all refugees.

We are simple and ordinary people

but we are living in tough times.

We are branded as refugees

but are we hateful?

Are our actions hateful?

The word *refugee* is not a hate-filled word

but, sadly, it angers many

And it makes their blood boil.

But let us assure you we are not bad people.

We do not steal, nor rob others.

Back in our border town,

the insurgents had been attacking us.

They killed many of our relatives

And it's just that fortune held our hands and helped us escape.

Yes, the word escape – it sounds like the gentle flow of the river.

But I tell you it isn't so.

It is not honey.

It contains our world of uncertainty, hunger and thirst.

It contains our memory of homes, homes destroyed;

the sweet smell of our country's soil; the smell of trees carried by the breeze.

"Yes, yes," some said. Others nodded. Some clapped.

We don't want global attention;

we only want our government to stop backing the insurgents

And we only desire that the government of this beautiful land

this glorious land that has seen two major wars

and stood with its heritage;

we only want the present government of this land where we are standing

to let the government of the land where we come from across the border,

feel the pain of our ruin.

This will help us relocate to our lands.

The success of this plan is not possible

without the support and collaboration of government agencies,
non-governmental organisations,
service providers and refugee communities
– many of whom, it is hoped are here today.

We hopped into a taxi, but a light blue fiat tailed us
and soon a hand shot out from the window
and aimed a gun.
And a bullet whizzed past my head
and cracked the window glass.
Our driver stepped on the gas,
swerved and screeched down
in double speed, turned straight and streaked ahead.

Slogan On Walls

Ghungroo's POV

Dad sent word for me and leaving everything
I rushed.
And he said, "Ghungroo, my girl
There is a certain Mr Rozario
his nephew has arrived from across the border."

Unce Rozario stood at the door, his jaws hung low,
forcing his mouth open.
I don't see your nephew, said I, looking behind him.

Uncle Rozario pointed to one of the rooms inside his house.
You know people are crossing the border every day.
Michael has arrived
along with innumerable people.

A handsome young man appeared at the door.

Sleeplessness had reduced his face
to a withered root
and dark rings below his eyes
and terror lurking in their sockets
and fearful memories stalking his mind.
Michael is Jozef's friend, uncle said.

Both of us were walking down a deserted road in Kimmings Raod,
Michael's voice was slow and drawling.
We were persuading Maria, Jozef's girlfriend
to cross the border and not remain emotionally attached
to a house where her parents and small brother were killed.
We stopped at a corner to urinate behind a tree,
and then we would go
to Maria's house at the other end of the street.
He stopped, searching in his mind
for the lost words.
The road was empty because the terrorists had earlier gunned down
all the inhabitants of the locality.
He stopped, his eyes growing larger.
Suddenly a jeep rushed down,

stopped and soldiers jumped out.
They entered one house after the other,
searching.
They came to the third house
and in an instant were dragging out Maria.
And they tore at her clothes, and... Michael stopped, horror written on his face.
Maria screamed, I picked up a fallen branch on the ground,
held it between my teeth to prevent myself from screaming.
Jozef screamed out and began running towards the miscreants.
Two of them lifted their automatic rifles calmly
and sprayed bullets into his chest
the ease of a professional inscribed on his attitude.
After the third soldier had finished, the other two lifted Maria,
put her into the jeep and sped away.

"Soldiers you say," Michelle asked.

"No. Terrorists. Disguised as soldiers."

Uncle Rozario made an endeavour to fight back his emotion
and Michelle held his hand

I placed my hand on his shoulder.

Some unexplainable pain, deeply lodged,
is visible in his heart.
The septuagenarian's well has dried up,
and all that his heart can produce
and display
is nothing more than a vacant stare.

I stood there for how long I did not know.
Uncle's touch on my hand
pushed me out of my thoughts,
uncle indicated us to follow him.

Little Happyland

Ghungroo's POV

The streets wore a quiet and sleepy look.
Some people moved about,
but this locality was a silent sufferer.
They were a voiceless
and tongue-tied pack of dogs
given up fighting
their death a few breaths away.
They feared
anxiety had lassoed their mantra of living.

The relatives of the run-away people, the *refugees,*
have given them shelter here.

In one corner of a lane,
three children
playing catching catch
their screams

their laughter
coated with fun.

Stepping into Free Avenue
a flutter reached our ears.
Our eyes went up, fell on a banner
strung from one side to the other
and in royal blue against a white background,
it fluttered.
Little Happyland.

My hand was on my face, my mouth gaped.
For some moments,
I searched for words but could not find any
and I clutched Michelle's arm.
When I looked at the rest,
everyone had a similar expression
written on their faces.

Slogan on the walls, in red, blue. And black.
 No Place For Insurgents
Common Lives Matter
We Want Peace.

Another one pasted on the wall of a house:
Mr. Insurgent, you have no place here.
We do not deal with bullets.
Sketches of some faces filled the wall.
And tar ran in blotches over the eyes,
dribbles of tar lines down the cheeks.

Uncle read our surprise.

"Yes, our haven, this," he said.

People followed uncle.

They were Michael and the affected residents of the neighbourhood.

Uncle came up closer to me.

"I've seen how the people are following you.

And if you say something to the people

they will be inspired."

I looked at Michelle.

She smiled

nodded.

Uncle handed me the mike.

Leaning against the wall of a house at the pavement, I started:

I stand here today, for I have been called with love.

Here, in your midst. (I pointed to the gathered people).

It is for you and you alone I stand here.

And from my heart will be born empathy for you;

and for your brothers and sisters.

Nobody likes to leave his country.

No one likes to be snatched away

from his mother's loving lap.

Your country is your mother.

But what has happened? And has been happening?

Many of you have been snatched away

from your mother's loving bosom.

You have crossed the border with fear in your hearts.

When a baby deer is lost in the forest,

and she looks here and there for his mother,

have you noticed the fear lurking in her kohl-black eyes?

Have you seen how lost the poor soul appears?

His little legs wobble at the knees,
his tiny heart jumps constantly.
You are no less a lost baby deer.
Some government officials have lain down traps
on the forest floor.
They have hung snap traps from the branches above.
As you will walk below it without knowing it is there,
the open mouth will snap in a flash,
hold you in lock-jaw and its cruel eyes smile.
These officials' mind is a jungle,
and you are trapped in it.
Many of your loving family members
and friends have been put to the sword.
And many who reside here have neither seen
nor heard any news of their relatives,
from their near and dear ones across the border.
I can feel the fearful beatings of their hearts
and the sleepless nights they encounter.
When you take shelter in a border country,
you are a refugee.
You have nowhere else to go
but wait for the government to inject sympathy.

The pavement becomes your home,
the open sky your ceiling,
and the same ceiling leaks during the rains;
and during summer it changes to a hot tin roof.
All we want is shelter from these natural calamities,
and security of our lives from the government.

I handed the mike over to the man.
"Bravo, Ghungroo," Uncle said, his voice quavering a little.
"See, you have so many followers.
And with your power of speech, we cannot wait
to be rid of the country's venom."

Ill Health

Ghungroo's POV

And as I ran my eyes through the news
and the cool breeze continued to blow
and brushed our faces in occasional zephyrs
it happened then.

I took a few steps forward, when out of the blue moonlight
my head swung, my body swayed
and in a reflex, Michelle grabbed my arm
and she dragged me to the pavement,
helped me rest against the shuttered door of a shop
looked up and down the road, biting her nails.
There, a rickshaw was arriving from Fern Road.

The little girl smiled in the calendar, her teeth a sparkle,
and she swung as a pendulum in the fan breeze,

a scratching noise behind the doctor's big padded chair.

The clinic was marginally full and a faint smell of medicine
hung in the air.
A small boy was leaning against his mother's arm,
playing with the gold bangles around her wrist.
An aged man in grey trousers was dozing
in one corner of the bench.

The doctor arrived after sometime, tall and heavily built,
his broad face serious.
He checked my wounds
he scanned at the few scabs on the arm,
and two peeping out from my armpits
and at the groin.

When you look at the sky, my friend,
and your mind rests on the grey lining
around the cloud
of an early monsoon,
that minute point of time

becomes another chapter of a story.

So I looked at the sky through the poky holes
of this pavement hut, my palace
and I viewed a larger sky, and a generous bunch of clouds sailing
like a fleet of ships
together on a voyage
towards the unknown.

And my days passed, one after another;
and one hope joined to another,
with the feel-good factor
for more than ten days,

I told my mind, let's sail,
and he took me on his magic cloud
the cool wind and the trees, the little cottage in Kurseong
from where you can see the plains of Siliguri
to your left
and Darjeeling to your right,
and if the view is uninterrupted

even by your soul

by an overcast sky,

the Kanchanjunga tip comes into view.

My medicines of the mind, I had them one by one,

and before the doctor's prescribed medicines were over,

I was a new being.

Energised.

Hopeful.

Mother Love

Foetus-bro's :POV

Foetus: My mother, she is my pillar

a brown pigeon among the black ones lining the parapet.

She turns her neck sideways, keeps it unmoving,

then in a languid style brings her head down

and dips her beak to the shoulder above her left wing,

and preens.

And she repeats the same method on the right.

A daily exercise.

The other birds of her tribe gawk,

and when the golden brown bird doesn't look at them,

they repeat her every action.

The males fly down and dance around her,

strutting their macho-ness.

My mother similar to this pigeon. My mother leads,

she is not lead.
She is tough.
She has toughened.

Even if war resounds in the surrounding area
and blazing guns boom out violence and anger,
and walls shatter and crumble and fall,
she will clutch on to her child.

Even if her house be burnt down to ashes
and her belongings demolished
and turned inside out,
and her money looted and squandered,
she will clutch on to her child.

She will clutch on to her child
with butchered body and severed arms,
powdered ribs and slit tongue.
She will clutch on to her child till her last breath flits away
and from her soul fades away the warmth of a springtime sky.

Ghungroo: Of course. Always there for you.

A Marriage

Ghungroo's POV

Michelle and I picked up two garlands of hibiscus
from among the framed pictures of Goddess Kali
in the makeshift stalls
scattered around the temple road
and a small container of vermillion
and a packet of incense sticks
with the fragrance of lavender.

And when we stepped inside
our feet felt the coolness of the temple floor
and the priest pulled us inside
and he eyed me and scratched his genitals
and he prayed to the goddess
and pictured his hand crawling over my dusky skin
from my throat travelling to the cleavage
down my waist.
And he blabbered mantras,

and from a small glass
hidden behind famed pictures
he drank some honey-colored liquid
in between his prayers
and he paused on a sudden
and opened the vermillion container
and taking his palm closer
held the container in front of our faces.

Michelle took a pinch of the powder
and when she had applied it on the central parting
of my hair
just above the forehead
the priest instructed me to do the same on Michells's forehead
and we put the garland of flowers
around each other's neck.

I looked into Michelle's eyes
and she into mine
and we smiled
a married smile.
At our dwelling I lay on the floor

my head on Michelle's lap
and the voice of a baul singer
on marriage and love
floated from the transistor
the voice reaching a crescendo.
And while it descended
the music from the ektara floated sharp and clear.

*

Foetus-bro POV

Sometimes night arrives and the joy
is the tinkling of anklets that accompanies the dancer
and yet, the activity of the day
in sombre grey etched in stone

Ghungroo leaned her head on Michelle's shoulder
and rested her lips on her cheek.
But no stir from Michelle,
and no more movement from Ghungroo
but two of them close, unmoving,
like a statue of immortal lesbian lovers
to be carved in stone and put up at the market square
where passersby will stop, taking a break from reaching their destination

and errand runners will recall the lovers' story
and after, plays will be enacted in theatres
and their story written and copies of the book
displayed in bookstores.

In schools and colleges their story will become a part
of the English syllabus
and haunting speeches will be memorized
and elocution contests will be held.

And their love story will be immortalised.

Is there any goddess for lesbian love?

But if there be one, it matters little.
What matters is fashioning a new one
and that is the Goddess Ghungroo-Michelle.
Their statue will be the still-moment of life
as they are now in their pavement dwelling. Together.

This Ghungroo-Michelle pose will be fashioned and put up

at the door of Mocambo's above the picture of the two beer jugs

tilted and touching each other in glory at the rim

the brown liquid pouring out in a still-life fashion

froth-topped.

And also at the lobby of Park Hotel's two upholstered single sofas

and another beside the potted Erica palm pouring out its leaves in all fertility.

And your poster will rise like a sea-nymph

at Shaw's one of the oldest bars at Metro Lane

above the noise of the waiters taking orders and money

before serving drinks asked by the customers.

And when the liquid will enter into their blood stream

and wander about and move towards their brain

the customers will stare at Ghungroo and Michelle

and take their imagination one step ahead of the poster

and they will stretch their mind and see Michelle

extending her hand towards her beloved

and see your face easing towards her

and your mouth opening

your mouth taking the finger in
the lips closing in all gentleness
and the saliva-ed tongue lapping the finger…

In that state of slowness called love,
in that state of her mind a meandering river now
Ghungroo turned Michelle's face and looked into her eyes.
And with her own drunk ones
she rested her lips on hers
she allowed her tongue to rule.
And so it snaked itself into Michelle's mouth
and Michelle unmoved, but as her emotion crept into her mind
and like a map spread out on the table, her passion covered her entire brain
she lay trapped by warmth from her huntress' love.

The night and the emotion called for a celebration.
No hotels they could go to
Dangerous it was to wander towards the streets
where parties took place
where all the celebrations of social gatherings were held.

As Ghungroo gestured and Michelle stood up

the honey light from the street lamp removed their clothes

and covered them with its nudity

and ahead, the pavements were a graveyard and the refugees asleep

covered with shrouds – so peaceful yet so vulnerable.

From a distance, the green gate was visible.

They went up the wooden stairs,

climbed the wooden railing and stepped on the wooden balcony.

And Michelle peeped from the glass window

as her mother lay on her side, a gentle snore puncturing the silence of the room

a shaft of moonlight on her leg from the western window.

The clock struck one, and they sat on the wooden floor

and Ghungroo hummed the latest baul song,

striking at the one-stringed ektara in rhythm

and Michelle strummed chords on her hollow guitar

when Ghungroo adjusted a tune here, added a sharp note there,

and took the scale to C flat

and as she cleared her throat, she hummed again.

In no time the song appeared etched clear in her mind

she began singing the lyrics and matching them with the rhythm of the tune.

And music from the two instruments and her voice

travelled into the deep and dark night.

Michelle strummed soft as ever

not with a gentle sweep of the edge of the thumbnail

but the soft fleshy pad of the thumb.

Strum. Strum. And strum.

Ghungroo's finger flickering on the one string

produced a murmur in the night

and it went into its darkness

marrying the lovers' story of love and pain

the female-female love

the Ghungroo-Michelle love

the Michelle-Ghnngroo love.

The immortal lesbian love.

Michelle added her voice into the refrain

their voice suppressed

their strumming soft.

And they looked at each other

and they got up, they took the two steps into the verandah.

Four strides and they were to the end of the balcony

and they climbed down.

Their silent footfalls fell on the wooden stairs.

A shaft of light from the street lamp

came filtering through the maze of the banyan tree leaves

and fell on the cemented stone steps of the neighbors

and choosing this as their bower they began again

their gentle sweep over the strings.

Ghungroo's finger flashed as it moved over the string

and sharp yet soft metallic sound and a twang at the fourth beat

as next to her, Michelle strummed

four times C Major

then a graceful shift of the middle and ring finger

and strummed A Minor, back to C Major.

The fingers then dived down to F, before they slipped to C-G7.

The music loud and clear

the mind heady as Michelle swooned to the strums

and Ghungroo sang out the words.

The words and the chords, and the sound of the ektara

moved in a blend of harmony and the music wept

when the singing paused after every refrain.

And the deep night watched.

The shadows of the leaves swayed to the weeping,

century summers old

weeping born in since the day of your birth

your birth to become a lesbian lover

since the first day of the world.

Ghungroo's voice went back to C major

and the song repeated one more time.

Eastland Is Happyland

Ghungroo's POV

The news in the daily, and over the radio:
Westland has been crushed,
and the country of the refugee people safe.
With peace and happiness
brushing its soft lips
on their soul
they can return
and hope
to build a new house,
a new-founded future founded on previous hopes.

Yelling of joy rang in the voices of the refugees
and from their food plates came metallic noises
when pieces of wooden batons struck.
And even the elders sang songs and the faces of the aged and frail
lit up into all teeth.

Michelle and I moved ahead, and there on the corner
in the midst of the yodeling and happy clamour
on the soot-covered pavement, a musty smell
lay trapped in the wooden crates
and cane baskets piled with unwashed clothes
and flies crowded around a blotch of saliva
like black-uniformed rugby players
bent in the centre field, head together,
holding on to each other's shoulders.

A woman in her early twenties
– a common face of a refugee –
lay on a piece of cloth.

Beads of perspiration spotted her forehead and cheeks
and some ran down like little silvery tracks
from her forehead.
Her legs bent at the knees, her body covered
with a fresh red-checked cotton towel.

On a sudden the thin wail of a baby

rose up above from the debris
the dirt of the road
sliced pieces of coconut shells
and on the ground between her drawn-up legs
a baby lay
a baby just born
its brown body in transparent slimes
and red blotches here and there.

The mother's face pale,
weakness surrounding all over,
and the radiance from her pale happy eyes
wielded a look of satisfaction.

An effort she made and craned her neck,
raising her head to eye her creation
and the umbilical cord through which travelled the food juices
the juices from the bits of vegetables
picked up from the market floor
and cooked over a slow fire
had all the little strength to the growth of the child.

But now the cord of the life-juice
needed separating
and she looked here and there
but found nothing.
No scalpel to cut the cord
no blade to slice the life-pipe.
The tube lay joining the mother and baby.

Her friends gave up their desperate search
and turned for some sharp object.
When nothing seemed around except dirt and stones
and sticks from a damaged wicker basket
a broken portion of brick said *I will help.*
With my crude sharp projections.

A determined friend took up the brick,
she struck at the cord, maroon-dark in color
the cord that had lain coiled all those months
inside the stomach like a viper
encased in a glass bottle of methylated spirit
was now straightened
and struck with the crude surgical weapon.

Strike! Strike! Till the affected part weakened.
The fibre loosened and became little pieces
and the woman struck again
the cord separated into two.

The first stage over, the second one loomed
like an obstacle and smiled a wicked smile.
No water! No water! The practical doctor looked around.
and she worked her tongue inside her mouth
and swabbed it around the teeth
till a sufficient amount of saliva formed
and she brought it near the tip of the tongue
and she formed a large blob
and she aimed it at the two new ends of the cord
and when the white mass filled with tiny bubbles fell
the fingers of her left hand rubbed the cord
and the saliva-filled fingers worked over with artistic intricacies
and they removed the grit of the pavement
and the minute *bricky* particles
and necessity really became the mother of invention.

A baby born on the day
a country broke the shackles of slavery.

The Other Dimension Or Ghungroo Dies

Ghungroo's POV

I pressed Michelle's hand and I spoke, my words halting:

A baby will be born from my womb.

A war baby.

A Pablo Picasso of Calcutta.

A Sylvia Plath of the pavement.

A Socrates of Calcutta.

Its father with a bastard mind

of Power and Oppression

the baby fatherless

and without a foster father

born of a virgin mind

a motherly mind.

*

They came.

They saw.

They spread me…
Julius Caesar would have applauded at the rephrase
and I smiled as I uttered the words.
My eyes were at the lamppost,
on the figure tied,
head bent over the right chest,
eyes closed.
The smell of the pavement wafted inside,
and it hung in the air.

*

"Yes, all these people,
they came one by one."

A soft noise at the curtain-door,
scratch-scratch,
scratch-scratch-scratch
and scratch again.
I lifted my eyes.
Michelle smiled, a soft smile it was;
and sitting beside me,
kept the packet of medicines
on the footstool.
I returned to polishing my nails.

"… and all of them, all spread me with aids…"

And Michelle wrapped her arms around me, her beloved.

"No, Ghungroo," she whispered. "None of the customers."

She gently ran her hand over my shoulder.

"And I can say this with conviction.

Because I handed them condoms when they paid money."

She waited for the words to sink in me.

"You contracted it when you were escaping from the border."

*

Ghungroo: Son, are you there?

Foetus: Yes, mother.

Ghungroo: I'm waiting for you.

See, when I will have applied the last touch

of nail polish

on my toenails,

my work in this earth will be done,

and I will get up on the rickshaw,

and you will ride me to the other dimension.

Come rickshaw
take me
transport me
transport your transit passenger.

My eyes close
a soft hand rests on my shoulder
my brother holds my hand
I get up
I turn to look
and there my body lies
still
unmoving.
A song hums out from his throat:

> *…it's getting' dark, too dark to see*
> *I feel I'm knockin' on Heaven's door.*

Ghungroo's Spirit Lives

A padlock, rusted by the rain
and summer heat,
bruised and blackened by nature's fury,
hangs on the door of the hovel.

Refugee children place their ears
at the door
and listen.
A voice from within
my voice:
I renamed myself Ghungroo.
One small anklet bell rolled down the table,
it produced a sweet sound.
And within my tiny heart
the gentle far-away peal stirred a feeling strange
a feeling defined yet undefined,
 a n*o* and *yes* at the same time.
The anklet-bell music played in my ears,
captured my heart.

I still recall the bountiful man gifting it,

fishing it out from his pocket

and unwrapping it, he held it close to the closeness

of my ears.

Once there, he shook it.

Peal-peal.

The gentle far-away sound,

a balm,

and my mind soothed.

And with the sound of peal in my ears,

I moved about in my little room,

that day,

on the pavement,

dancing a jig;

muttered the name in my mind;

click-clacked my tongue every now and then.

A mixed feeling of pleasure

and no-pleasure

on my soft cheeks danced

with the name

I had rechristened.

And thus Ghungroo was born.

This is not an Epilogue, but
A Pact Between You And Me

Before I begin to collect my notes, before I arrange the pages, number them page one, two, three, let me tell you, my friend, he is coming to take me away. He stays close to my residence, and has never broken his promise.

So that you trust me, so that I will go without any regret, I have taken this task of arranging these sheets. And as I do, I will read out to you, to ensure that if you have some doubts, some questions playing hide and seek in your mind, you may feel free and ask me, I will clarify them. Thus, after having heard the journey of my life, you may give me a clean chit, clear me of blame and erase any doubt from tugging at your conscience. Because this happens to be the first time I have ever hidden anything from you.

There, on the little cane table, your favourite pizza, Neapolitan Pizza, ordered online from Dominos counter, New Empire. They have topped it with tomato, garlic, oregano and extra-virgin olive oil. I insisted them to add two slices of bacon, your treasured salt-cured meat over it. So that as you listen, you will take bites in between and sip orange juice prepared in the fruit-juice mixer by me.

About the Author

Bob DCosta

Bob is a poet, novelist and consulting educationist with several books of poems, novels in paperback and in e-book form and two novels in Dreame. He has worked as a school teacher for two decades but now runs a humble institute teaching English to children as well as giving talks on Happiness that can be achieved by living a simple life, minimum wants and living one day at a time, that is, living for the Now. Bob lives in Kolkata but dreams of mountain mist floating through the open window and bringing the soft peals of bells from the Buddhist temple into his room. He is a member of Foundation of SAARC Writers and Literature, the SAARC Apex Body.

Praise for Bob DCosta's work

"A writer with a different voice, Bob DCosta grips the reader from the very first page."

Paroma

"Poetic and fresh, *The Indian Crow* captures the unseen and unfelt emotions of the lower middle class of eastern India, and their desperate attempt to claim intellectual oneness with the idea of democracy. The prose is tender, the concept unique, and the satire razor sharp."

Kulpreet Yadav, Author & motivational speaker

"Bob DCosta's poems are real poetry. Poetry of Walt Whitman, Lorca, Pablo Neruda, Majaz, Mayakovsky, Sardar Jafri and Faiz Ahmed Faiz."

K. A. Abbas, Indian film director, screenwriter, novelist and a journalist

"This poet's themes are taken from the Calcutta streets; he is moved by the poverty and disease of his fellow citizens. A remarkable achievement."

Jayanta Mahapatra, Poet Winner of Shahitya Academy Award

"Bob DCosta is a poet of many excellences. He is the Federick Lorca of India."

> **Dr Krishna Srinivas, President, World Poetry Society, Intercontinental. Co-Founder, World Congress of Poets**

"Just like Bob Dylan, Bob DCosta too can see through the masks of which we are all a part of struggling every day for a new brotherhood."

> **Dr Rosemary C. Wilkinson, Secretary General, World Academy of Arts and Culture, California**

www.ingramcontent.com/pod-product-compliance
Lightning Source LLC
LaVergne TN
LVHW041937070526
838199LV00051BA/2818